Para la Gente

Art, Politics, and Cultural Identity of the Taller de Gráfica Popular

Selected Works from the Charles S. Hayes Collection of Twentieth-Century Mexican Graphics

Gina Costa
Lauren Henderson
Lauren Magnifico
Mary Cecilia Mitsch
Lindsay Poulin
Nicole Paxton Sullo

Snite Museum of Art
University of Notre Dame

CONTENTS

ACKNOWLEDGMENTS AND INTRODUCTION FROM THE AUTHOR

In 2005, the Snite Museum of Art received an important loan of works, which is now a generous gift to the Museum, from Charles S. Hayes, Notre Dame 1965 graduate. This collection came to be the Charles S. Hayes Collection of 20th-Century Mexican Graphics.

The images selected for this publication are drawn from this collection and survey the work by the Taller de Gráfica Popular, a workshop of politically engaged artists working in Mexico City from 1937 until about 1953, when they informally disbanded and were drawn into other programs, organizations or individual projects.

These artists worked in a period of immense political change as well as rich artistic activity. Their work reflects the issues of postrevolutionary Mexico's political and social upheaval. The political posters, broadsides, books, and political announcements created illustrate the TGP's direct and powerful style as well as their deep commitment and response to the agenda of political reforms that were part of the Cárdenista government in Mexico at that time.

This publication and accompanying exhibition attempt to advance growing interest in and scholarship about the artists of the Taller de Gráfica Popular by offering their interpretation of the dignity of the human condition in the context of the social reform movements of the time. Their depictions and representations of workers and farmers, and the social struggles of the people mark the TGP as important revolutionary agents in their own right.

It is not the intent of this publication to provide exhaustive interpretive analysis of the images presented, duplicating fine work already done by scholars in the field. Rather, the objective is to offer readers and viewers of the exhibition an introduction to the political context in which the works were created, and selective analysis of various prints as an example of how these artists used their media as a vehicle for social change.

In selecting the works from the Charles S. Hayes Collection to include in this exhibition and catalogue, my assistants and I studied the hundreds of prints in the collection. Great care was taken to select a variety of examples which best tell the story of these remarkable artists and the politically charged time in which they worked.

I would like to thank Charles S. Hayes '65 for generously gifting this collection of over 560 works of the Taller de Gráfica Popular to the Snite Museum of Art.

Heartfelt thanks to Nicole Paxton, Higgins Graduate Intern, for her unparalleled contributions to this publication. Nicole and Lauren Magnifico, Saint Mary's College '06, who kept the early years of this project on course, were invaluable assistants. Thanks also to undergraduate assistant Lauren Henderson, who tracked down hard-to-find historical information, doing an impressive job every step of the way. Very special thanks go to Michael Swoboda, MA '08 graphic designer, who designed this handsome publication and exhibition and who, along with Lauren Magnifico, shared with me his enthusiasm and keen sense of humor. Thanks also to Mary Cecilia Mitsch and Chris Andrews for their contributions. It was with great joy that I worked with my student assistants and interns.

I am indebted to Sarah Tremblay for editing the manuscript. Her gracious and generous comments were invaluable.

Special thanks to Gerta Katz who shared hours of phone interviews about her and her husband Samuel's time in Mexico working with the TGP. It was in 2004 that Charles Hayes acquired the Gerta and Samuel Katz collection of Mexican Graphics, which included 111 prints and 5 portfolios, forming the core of the Hayes TGP collection.

Thanks also to Master Photographer Antonio Turok who provided invaluable insight into the political dimension of the time in Mexico; to Miguel Zuniga for his assistance in locating hard-to-find publications and interviews in Mexico City; to Master Printer Joe Segura for his generosity in sharing interview transcriptions he had conducted with Jules Heller; and to Katie and Noah Kahn who shared reminiscences of their parents' (Eleanor Coen and Max Kahn) time in Mexico working with the TGP.

Thanks also to my Snite Museum colleagues: Ramiro Rodriguez, exhibitions coordinator, Eric Nisly, digital archivist and photographer, and John Phegley, exhibition designer for their generous assistance.

And finally, thanks to Snite Museum Director Charles Loving for giving me the opportunity to share this collection with the public.

— Gina Costa

Curator of the Charles S. Hayes Collection of 20th-Century Mexican Graphics

May 7, 2009

ACKNOWLEDGMENT FROM THE DIRECTOR OF THE SNITE MUSEUM OF ART

The Snite Museum of Art, University of Notre Dame, takes great pride and pleasure in exhibiting and publishing highlights of the Charles S. Hayes Collection of Twentieth-Century Mexican Graphics.

Hayes's generous gift of over 500 prints produced by the Taller de Gráfica Popular (TGP) furthers the Museum's ambition to create one of our nation's finest collections of Latino art. That collection features premier pre-Columbian artworks, examples of Spanish Colonial art, Latin American photography of the 19th through 21st centuries, modest holdings of Modern Latino paintings and prints, and extensive examples of contemporary Chicano prints (courtesy of Gilberto Cardenas).

Therefore, we are extremely grateful to ND alum Charles Hayes '65 for his most recent benefaction which adds strength and depth to Latino holdings within the Modern period.

I appreciate Gina Costa's effective oversight of all aspects of receiving, documenting, exhibiting and interpreting the Hayes collection. Her essay provides a valuable grounding in the TGP and associated Mexican social and political history. She also shares new insight into connections between Chicago artists and the TGP. This was a labor of love for Costa, and I am thankful for her unflagging dedication to the Hayes Collection.

The Museum also appreciates the services of the individuals acknowledged in Costa's introduction, who were essential to the success of this endeavor which underscores art's principal values. That is, exhibitions such as this one assist societies and their individual members in understanding who they are, their common values, and what they aspire to become. It also demonstrates how people from different cultures, as well as individuals within the same society, differently perceive their physical, social, political and spiritual worlds.

— Charles R. Loving

Director and Curator, George Rickey
Sculpture Archive

May 30, 2009

Para la Gente

Art, Politics, and Cultural Identity of the Taller de Gráfica Popular

Selected Works from the Charles S. Hayes Collection of Twentieth-Century Mexican Graphics

1. INTRODUCTION

The Taller de Gráfica Popular (Popular Graphic Arts Workshop), or TGP, an important group of printmakers founded in Mexico City in 1937, created political prints and posters designed to galvanize audiences both in Mexico and around the world. As their country emerged from the Mexican Revolution, a bloody civil war that had pitted impoverished workers against wealthy landowners, these artists produced and circulated thousands of images that expressed the need for social and political reform for the Mexican oppressed. Their extremely successful public art highlighted the unjust treatment of farmers and peasants and satirized political abuses and excesses, reinforcing the reform movements initiated by the government during and after the revolution. In Mexico, prints had historically served as a critical tool in the struggle for social justice. The Taller continued this tradition of using graphic art as an agent of change, creating a public consciousness about the political and social state of the country.

The Mexican Revolution had broken out in 1910 as a resistance to the 1876–1910 dictatorship of Porfirio Díaz, known as the Porfiriato. During Díaz's presidency, 75 percent of the Mexican people lived in extreme poverty in rural conditions, with little or no access to education. Although his policies fostered this huge disparity among the social classes, Díaz did bring certain advances to the country. He developed the economy, especially through the construction of factories, roads, and industries, promoting the influx of foreign capital from countries such as

England and France. His greatest achievement was the laying out of the Mexican railroad system. Díaz's mistake, however, was that he accomplished these projects at the expense of the working classes, who suffered extreme exploitation. Wealth, political power, access to education, and ownership of land remained concentrated among a handful of families, mostly of European descent, who invested in these modernization programs.

In 1910, Francisco I. Madero and the now-legendary revolutionaries Francisco "Pancho" Villa and Emiliano Zapata came together in a joint effort to rebel against Díaz and his policies on behalf of the oppressed population. A ten-year period of fighting ensued. Villa commanded revolutionary forces from the north, while Zapata commanded forces from the south. Both men became renowned for fighting for the return of land to the poor and for promoting educational and cultural reforms. Eventually, these revolutionary leaders were assassinated, Zapata in 1919 and Villa in 1923. Madero ran for the presidency against Díaz in 1910, winning by a landslide and providing the momentum for the outbreak of the revolution. However, he too was assassinated in 1913.

Even as the various generals and revolutionary leaders fought against one another for control, they also promoted reforms to redistribute land, construct public schools, advance education, and rewrite the constitution. The new constitution, fathered in 1917 by President Venustiano Carranza, helped to bring an

The current headquarters of the Taller de Gráfica Popular, in Mexico City, as it looks today.
Photo courtesy of Miguel and Isabella Zuniga

TGP artist Arturo García Bustos in his studio in Mexico City in 2009. *Photo courtesy of Miguel and Isabella Zuniga*

end to the civil war in 1920. It abolished the unfair landowning, educational, and political structures established during the Porfiriato, providing the foundation for Mexico's modern-day constitution. Still, political instability and unrest continued for some time under a succession of governments. Carranza was assassinated in 1920 in a coup by Alvero Obregón, who was president from 1920 to 1924, was reelected in 1928, and was himself assassinated later that year. In 1934, Lázaro Cárdenas became president. Shortly after taking control, in 1936 he arrested his predecessor, Abelardo Rodríguez (president from 1932 to 1934), as well as dozens of other corrupt politicians and generals, and deported them to the United States. Cárdenas was greatly admired by the Mexican people for his progressive ideas and numerous social reforms, including his initiatives to reallocate land to the peasants, reinstitute unions, establish higher wages, and nationalize foreign oil companies. Many think that the end of his presidency in 1940 marked the conclusion, at last, of the Mexican Revolution.[1]

The Taller de Gráfica Popular emerged during Cárdenas's presidency. Their images documented and supported his reforms and celebrated the end of years of unjust treatment of the Mexican people. The workshop grew out of an earlier group of artists and writers known as the Liga de Escritores y Artistas Revolucionarios (League of Revolutionary Writers and Artists), or LEAR. Many members of the LEAR had been part of the Estridentistas (Stridentist) movement during the 1920s, a collective of avant-garde artists, writers, and other intellectuals who shared an artistic vision. Building on the ideals of the Estridentistas, the LEAR sought a unified theory of cultural and political artistic expression utilizing the various styles of modern European art. When the group dissolved because of internal factional disputes in 1937, former members Leopoldo Méndez, Pablo O'Higgins, and Luis Arenal founded the Taller de Gráfica Popular. The Taller's bold, politically charged prints and broadsides would achieve international fame, attracting artists from the United States and elsewhere who shared their

interest in using art to effect social change and who came to Mexico City to find new sources of inspiration. The core members of the TGP would remain together until about 1953, at which time they informally disbanded and were drawn into other programs, organizations, and individual projects.

Jules and Gloria Heller on their Honeymoon in Mexico.
Photo courtesy of the Joe Segura, Travis Janssen, and the Heller Family

The well-known New York teacher, printmaker, and author Jules Heller and his wife Gloria, combined their honeymoon with a stint as visiting artists at the Taller. Here, Heller recounts his time working with the TGP and his memories of founder Leopoldo Méndez:[2]

My first reaction to the Taller was sort of meeting lost brothers, who were really committed to making prints. A number of them were teachers. They had gotten together because if you're a printmaker you have to have access to a press, obviously, and to equipment that most individuals don't have. They, I think, thank God for the presence of Leopoldo Méndez who spent about a year finding about 50 lithographic stones and a press that had a great big plaque on the front of it, on the yoke, that said 1871, and he was convinced that Daumier had printed on that press, because it came from Paris. When we were there in 1947, the Taller de Gráfica Popular *was in an apartment building, and was composed of three rooms. One was a room in which printmakers engraved linoleum or copper or wood or whatever or* worked on a lithographic stone. The second room, or one of the rooms, was filled with portfolios of the individuals' private works. And the third room was where the press was and all of its equipment and all the necessary peripheral stuff for printing took place. So it was always three rooms, and remember, they moved from one place to another because they had to pay rent and it was never very profitable . . . They did prints that referred to local phenomena, like a strike, like helping agricultural workers get higher pay. All the social and political phenomena of the day became the content, the essence of their black and white prints . . . They were all, to varying degrees, what we call progressive politically and socially, . . . they were all committed to what we could call left-wing politics, and specifically directed to the Mexican experience . . . They did group projects. They would decide on a theme . . . on Friday nights the group would get together, in terms of this group project, one at a time you'd put the present state of your work in the middle of the floor, and people would gather round and look at it. And whether you were eighteen years old or you were the well-known Leopoldo Méndez, all questions and all comments were welcome and acc... maybe not accepted, but they were all welcome.

Leopoldo and the group saw the purpose of the Taller . . . always believed and said, "These (prints they produced) were a weapon . . . I'm talking about the collective of the Taller." He said, "Art is a weapon. You can use it constructively, destructively; you can use it in a zillion ways. The Taller, as I (Jules) mentioned earlier, tried to use it constructively to educate, to propagandize, to reveal an attitude that they as a group had toward a specific problem in society. They had the courage and the wherewithal, because of the equipment and tools and the talent.

Printmaking had a long tradition in Mexico as the most effective tool of social commentary and political protest. The intersection of graphic art and political propaganda that defined the work of the TGP had been part of the country's visual vocabulary since the time of José Guadalupe Posada (1852–1913), the father of the modern Mexican print. Posada was the preeminent printmaker in prerevolutionary Mexico, producing more than fifteen thousand prints in his lifetime and gaining fame as a kind of popular hero in the 1920s. His bold, simplified, and direct manner of communicating his political views, and his deep commitment to the indigenous people, had a profound influence on the work and ideology of the TGP. Prints were effective tools because they could be quickly and cheaply mass-produced and because they presented clear messages that could easily be disseminated to an often-illiterate public (plate 3). The Taller artists generally used wood blocks and linoleum cuts, which favored a simple and direct working method. Their straightforward and expressive style, marked by strong angular outlines, dramatic light and dark contrasts, and easily recognizable imagery, ultimately became the workshop's trademark.

One of the primary objectives of the Taller's politically charged prints was to provide visual imagery supporting Cárdenas's socialist government, as well as the Communist party abroad.[3] Most of the TGP artists, with the exception of Alfredo Zalce, were members of the Mexican Communist party. Unlike in the United States, Communism was a fundamental philosophy that was historically part of the political, social, and cultural thinking in Mexico. The Taller was sympathetic to European antifascist causes and supported European exiles in Mexico who had emigrated for political reasons. Many of the posters the artists created addressed the spread of fascism, Nazism, and militaristic regimes such as that of pre-World War II Japan (plate 4). This engagement with issues of social justice beyond Mexico's own borders contributed to the international appeal of the Taller's images and the global reputation of the group.

2. POLITICAL & CULTURAL CONTEXT OF THE TGP

To understand the importance of the Taller Gráfica de Popular and the images its artists produced, one must consider the political and cultural context in which they worked. Artists do not live in a vacuum; their works, generally speaking, respond to, criticize, and comment on the social, political, and cultural conditions of their time. The TGP came together with the very specific intention of documenting and commenting on the social and political reforms of the Cárdenas presidency. As a result of their intense involvement with these issues, the workshop's members became not only agents of social change within Mexico but perhaps the most important group of politically motivated artists in modern art history.

The Taller's powerful prints depicted subjects ranging from the harsh and oppressive conditions of the peasant class to the atrocities of war, social injustices resulting from corrupt capitalism, and international political conflicts. These images ultimately served to reinforce the progressive policies of President Cárdenas. From the age of eighteen, Lázaro Cárdenas had fought for various Mexican revolutionary armies. In 1925, the twenty-nine-year-old was appointed brigadier general, becoming the youngest person ever to hold that rank in the Mexican army. By the time he was elected governor of Michoacán in 1928, Cárdenas had earned the affectionate nickname "Tata Cárdenas" (Dear Uncle Cárdenas) (plate 7). As governor, he worked to bring about the unrealized goals of the Mexican Revolution, such as the redistribution of land among peasants and the construction of new roads and schools. During his two terms as president, from 1934 to 1940, Cárdenas showed his concern "for the people" by cutting his salary in half and living in his own house instead of in the presidential palace. In 1938, he nationalized foreign oil companies, helping Mexico to become more economically independent. Cárdenas knew the potential of art as a vehicle for political propaganda, and he encouraged the establishment of the TGP as a national printing group to give visual expression to his progressive ideals.

By mass-producing bold, simple images, the TGP successfully communicated with the Mexican people and served as their advocate (plate 9). The effective combination of illustration and narrative text typical of their posters had its roots not only in the work of Mexico's masterful political printmaker José Guadalupe Posada but also in the early twentieth-century Soviet *agitprop* poster movement, which used art as propaganda to support Communist policies. The Taller were not the only artists in Mexico working toward social reform; at this same time, the revolutionary Mexican muralists Diego Rivera, José Orozco, and David Siqueiros were producing large-scale wall paintings celebrating the class struggle of the Mexican worker. Their iconic images revealed a new cultural ideology commemorating the *mestizo* (mixed European and Amerindian) heritage that had been lost prior to the revolution, under Porfirio Díaz. In a similar vein, the TGP artists created images that could easily be pasted on walls and signboards and distributed in broadside form throughout Mexico City to promote discussion of urgent cultural and political issues of the day. Like the muralists, they often put their art at the service of specific contemporary movements for social justice; for example, they supported local agricultural workers' unions and endorsed national literacy programs (plate 10). Their prints also delved into broad issues such as the corruption of contemporary politicians, the profascist biases of the so-called free press, and the conflict between the church and the state. These images had the effect of fueling public outrage over abuses and gathering support for the reforms that were the direct outcome of the revolution (plates 11, 12).

In addition to directly addressing contemporary social issues, the TGP's prints traced the history of the Mexican Revolution as a means of promoting their reformist ideals, often using satire and caricature to convey their message. One of their most comprehensive works on this topic was a folio entitled *Estampas de la Revolución Mexicana*. Conceived in the early

1940s and completed in 1947, this collaborative project comprises eighty-five prints designed as social and political commentary on the revolution (plate 17).[4] It was also an income-generating venture for the group, made possible in part by the direction of Hannes Meyer, a former director of the Bauhaus school in Germany who was instrumental in the 1940–43 reorganization of the TGP and the establishment of an in-house publishing company, La Estampa Mexicana.[5] The folio is loosely organized into four thematic sections: the revolution, the postrevolutionary phase, the administrations of the 1920s and early 1930s, and the government from 1940 to 1947. The historical events commemorated in each print are explained at the beginning of the collection in the *Indice de los grabados con notas históricas*, written by Alberto Morales Jiménez. As the folio progresses, the prints alternately espouse the heroic virtues of revolutionaries such as Francisco Madero, Pancho Villa, and Emiliano Zapata and vilify the immorality and corruption of dictators such as Porfirio Díaz and Victoriano Huerta. President Cárdenas is portrayed as the redeemer of Mexico.

Francisco Madero was one of the main protagonists of the revolution, best known for "freeing" Mexico from Porfirio Díaz's dictatorship and its cruel treatment of the Mexican people. Taking a stand against Díaz, Madero wrote the inflammatory book *La sucesión presidencial en 1910* and formed the Partido Nacional de Antireeleccionistas. His actions motivated a revolutionary spirit in the public, who nominated him to run for the presidency in April 1910 (plate 13). After fleeing to San Antonio to escape arrest by Díaz, Madero declared himself a revolutionary president and promised to redistribute the lands usurped by Díaz. He officially ascended to the presidency on November 6, 1911, but his administration ended abruptly when General Victoriano Huerta first forced his resignation and then had him assassinated in February 1913.[6] Huerta went on to be a brief but oppressive dictator of Mexico.

The years that followed the violent first phase of the Mexican Revolution (1910–20) saw a series of social and political reforms established. The constitution that had been drafted in 1917 had facilitated the end of the war, and the military figures who had dominated the revolution's conflicts began to form political parties. Out of the many factions that had existed up until 1920, one culture—one nation was coming together. In 1920, Álvaro Obregón, the leading general to then-president Venustiano Carranza, conducted a successful coup against Carranza. Elected to the presidency in December of that year, Obregón ushered in a period of calm and stability. He also set into motion the reforms of the important 1917 constitution, which he had shared a crucial role in developing (plate 15). Establishing minimum and maximum wages, restraining the role of the Catholic Church, reforming education, and redistributing land to peasants were some of the improvements Obregón put into place. In 1924, Plutarco Elías Calles, Obregón's close friend, assumed the presidency, continuing many of the reforms enacted by his predecessor. Obregón decided to run again in 1928. By his second term as president, he had developed an adversarial relationship with the Catholic Church, resulting from his earlier efforts to enforce the articles of the 1917 constitution that limited the church's power; he would ultimately be assassinated (plate 16).[7] Like the early events of the revolution, these historical developments were documented in the TGP's images.

The cultural climate of the 1930s was just as important to the TGP's development and character as was the political climate. It was during this period that the concept of Mexicanidad (Mexicanness) was born. This idea expressed, reestablished, and celebrated all aspects of Mexican culture, history, and heritage. Before the revolution, Porfirio Díaz had endeavored to Europeanize Mexican culture. Seeking to do away with the rich artistic and cultural traditions that defined the Mexican people, Díaz looked to European, especially French, models to shape the country. It was only with his ultimate resignation and exile and the election of Francisco Madero to the presidency in the early years of the revolution that Mexicans once again began to rediscover their vibrant heritage. Mexicanidad sought to reverse the prevailing European models and reinvigorate the people's ethnic identity. This effort led to a newfound freedom and an explosion of artistic expression, setting into motion a renaissance in Mexican art. Teachers, activists, anthropologists, filmmakers, and artists joined in the campaign to reclaim and champion their cultural legacy. The movement sought to unite all Mexicans, not just the intellectuals or the wealthy but also the poor and indigenous. No longer did European models and styles set the standard for Mexican culture; Mexicans now looked to their own patrimony for a sense of identity. As a more united national consciousness evolved, the arts community sought to reexamine and redefine its heritage and its role in this new cultural character (plate 18).

In 1920, José Vasconcelos was appointed director of the Universidad Nacional. A philosopher, writer, and politician, Vasconcelos had a significant influence on the intellectual thought throughout Mexico. He created the Ministerio de Educación to address the problems of widespread illiteracy and lack of education for the poor. Vasconcelos was responsible for bringing art, music, and classical literature to the Mexican people. He enlisted artists in a national program, ushering in a flourishing of the arts during the 1920s and '30s. It was at this time that the murals of Los Tres Grandes (the Three Big Ones)—Diego Rivera, José Clemente Orozco, and David Alfaro Siqueiros—captured the imagination of the world. Vasconcelos's idea was to educate the people by using paintings on walls, posters and prints, and other easily disseminated and accessible media to bring the arts to all Mexican people. Images celebrating important events in Mexican history and politics reinvigorated and reinforced the Mexican people's sense of pride in their

history and traditions. The TGP artists, along with the mural painters and the important photographers who were working in Mexico City during this time, participated in this effort to document and celebrate Mexico's cultural and political achievements.

As a result, Mexico City became a vibrant center of artistic activity beginning in the mid-1920s. Artists, writers, and intellectuals from all over the world converged on the city. American artists Edward Weston, Marsden Hartley, and Paul Strand and Italian photographer Tina Modotti were just a few of those who traveled there. Leftist sympathizers found a likeminded community in Mexico City, as did European intellectuals trying to escape the growing fascist and Nazi terror at home. With their leftist politics and their intellectual ambivalence toward religion and government supremacy, avant-garde European artists found refuge in the fertile cultural soil of postrevolutionary Mexico. In the United States, foundations such as the Simon Guggenheim Memorial Foundation sent American artists to Mexico as part of a larger cultural exchange program. Painters, photographers, and writers all traveled to the country seeking its freedom of ideas.

POSADA AND THE CALAVERA

The politically minded graphic artists who formed the TGP are generally regarded as the artistic heirs to the great Mexican printmaker José Guadalupe Posada. Born in the early 1850s, Posada lived at a tumultuous time in Mexico's history. During Posada's childhood, the liberal Benito Juárez commanded a governmental revolt, and after becoming president he enacted many reforms in the country's constitution. By 1876, though, the political climate of the country changed drastically with the oppressive dictatorship of Porfirio Díaz.[8] Influenced by these events, Posada initiated what became a tradition of making satirical prints, which appeared in newspapers, journals, and editorial cartoons, often based on contemporary events. He is best known for his broadsides and *calaveras*— living skeletons that served as a substitute for the human figure in order to comment on political and social issues.

With roots in pre-Columbian imagery, *calaveras* enabled Posada's prints to resonate with Mexican viewers by referencing longstanding folk traditions. The artist used these skeletal caricatures to satirize all strata of Mexican society, but especially the upper class, public figures, and government officials. They demonstrated that, although there may be great discrepancy between the hardships of the poor and the luxuries of the wealthy in life, ultimately death equalizes the classes. Posada's works had an enormous influence on generations of subsequent artists both in Mexico and in the United States. Even today, the Chicano art movement is indebted to his humorous, biting satires of social and political injustices.[9] And *calaveras* are still a pervasive image in Mexican culture, most commonly depicted in early November during celebrations for the Día de los Muertos (Day of the Dead). Leopoldo Méndez was one of Posada's greatest admirers (plates 19, 21). He wrote extensively on the master's work, creating one of the most iconic images of him.

A detail of *Concierto Sinfónico de Calaveras* by Leopoldo Méndez shows the influence of *calavera* figures within the work of the TGP artists.

3. THE TALLER DE GRÁFICA POPULAR AND CHICAGO

The Taller de Gráfica Popular's artwork commented on social issues and political events not only in Mexico but also in the United States and elsewhere. During the 1930s and '40s, the United States was experiencing its own political and economic turmoil. The events of the Great Depression and World War II led to an American interest in socially conscious art that aligned with the Mexican artists' agenda (plate 30). The economic conditions of the Depression had special implications for artists, art programs and institutions, and welfare services all over the country. It was during this time that the Works Project Administration (WPA) and the Farm Security Administration (FSA) were born, in an attempt to put unemployed people, including artists, back to work. Many American photographers, especially those employed by Roy Stryker at the FSA, sought to record the plight of the American farmer and laborer. Dorothea Lange's powerful and moving photograph *Migrant Mother*, of 1936, is still considered the seminal visual symbol of this desperate time in America. The goal of these artists was the same as that of the TGP in Mexico: to become agents of social change by documenting the conditions of poverty and suffering. As a result of this shared concern, a rich and important connection developed between artists in Mexico and in the United States, who often traveled to each others' countries to study and work.

Interviews that I have conducted with surviving artists, their families and children, and others who worked with the Taller de Gráfica Popular suggest that Chicago, more than any other American city, had a special relationship with the workshop.[10] To date, no study has fully explored the TGP's significant relationship with Chicago artists and art institutions. While it is outside the scope of this publication to fully address this topic, I would like to briefly survey the relationship here. Chicago was uniquely positioned to be receptive to socially committed Mexican artists working in the United States. While New York City was the artistic center of the country and Los Angeles had ethnic ties with Mexico, Chicago was distinguished by its working-class roots, its political unions that fought for the rights of workers, and its down-to-earth, unpretentious work ethic. Alfredo Zalce explained to friend and art collector Gerta Katz that because of these qualities, the city offered an artistic environment that paralleled that of Mexico City and appealed to Mexico's politically and socially engaged artists. Zalce was among the many Mexican artists who spent significant time in the city, exhibiting, teaching, and producing art.

The likeminded spirit worked both ways: politically and socially minded artists in Chicago simultaneously looked to Mexico as a safe and receptive place to work—especially toward the end of the 1940s as the age of McCarthyism, with its intense anticommunist suspicion, commenced. It was in part the reorganization of the Taller around 1940–43, under the new leadership of Hannes Meyer, that made Mexico City so attractive to American artists. Like many Jewish artists, Meyer, a former director of the Bauhaus school in Dassau, fled Germany to escape Nazi persecution. Instead of joining many of his colleagues in the United States, he accepted Leopoldo Méndez's invitation to come to Mexico City to work with and lead the TGP. Postrevolutionary Mexico proved an ideal political climate for leftist, socially conscious, and Jewish refugees, including an influx of such artists from Chicago.

Added to this was the aesthetic and intellectual love affair with all things Mexican that swept the American imagination beginning in the 1920s. This was partially due to the representation of important Mexican artists in galleries and exhibitions, first in

New York City, Chicago, and Milwaukee, and soon in other parts of the United States. The Weyhe Gallery in New York City bought and exhibited works by Tamayo, Siqueiros, Rivera, Orozco, and others throughout the 1920s, '30s, and '40s.[11] Additionally, as early as 1916, Rivera participated in group shows at other U.S. art venues. In 1932, the Milwaukee Art Institute held a two-man exhibition of Leopoldo Méndez's and Carlos Mérida's works. The presence of the Mexican muralists' and printmakers' politically-charged works in the United States, combined with Americans' own romanticized mythologies, fueled individual artists' desire to look south of the border for a cultural tradition that merged art and politics. During this time and through World War II, the U.S. government also sponsored cultural exchange programs with Mexico (and the rest of Latin America), in an effort to consolidate the loyalty of its southern neighbor as an ally.

Chicago artists Eleanor Coen (Coney), Max Kahn, Morris Topchevsky, Charles White, and Mariana Yampolsky were among those who fell under the spell of the Mexican muralists and printmakers. They and others traveled to Mexico City to directly experience the TGP. For example, Chicago social documentary photographer Milton Rogovin (originally from Buffalo, New York) and his wife Anne went to Mexico in the early 1950s, meeting and working with members of the TGP, particularly Raul Angúiano. Rogovin was known in the United States for his socially critical images, and he photographed the poor and indigenous cultures in Mexico with the intent of circulating his images to American audiences. He found a strong kindred spirit in the work he encountered at the Taller. Acquiring some of their prints, he brought the works back to Chicago and shared them with his colleagues and the art world there—thus furthering the American fascination with the group.

THE ART INSTITUTE OF CHICAGO

The Art Institute of Chicago played an important role in bringing Mexican art to the city. In 1943, under the advice of then curator of prints and drawings Carl O. Schniewind, the AIC acquired the collection of Mexican prints formed by its famed curator Katherine Kuh, whose private Chicago gallery featured European, American Modernist, Mexican, and Latin American art. This acquisition formed the basis of the Art Institute's holdings of Mexican art—one of the most significant collections of Mexican prints at that time. The AIC acquired most of its prints by Leopoldo Méndez, Alfredo Zalce, Jesús Escobedo, Angel Bracho, Raul Angúiano, and Francisco Dosamantes, as well as works by Diego Rivera and José Clemente Orozco, during this period.

In 1944, Kuh organized at the Art Institute the first comprehensive exhibition of José Guadalupe Posada's work in the United States. Through this show, the American public began to understand the deep and complex relationship Mexican printmaking had with the cultural and political agenda of that nation. This 1944 exhibition at the AIC was followed by another in 1945, organized by Schniewind, featuring the prints and drawings of Leopoldo Méndez (plate 36). This print by Méndez is a complex self-portrait commissioned by Carl O. Schniewind for his 1945 exhibition at the AIC. Schniewind had previously gone to Mexico to visit the TGP, purchasing works by several artists with the intention of exhibiting them back in Chicago. Méndez created this piece for Schniewind while working in Chicago.

CHICAGO'S HULL HOUSE

Katherine Kuh's enthusiasm for and promotion of Mexican art in Chicago was not confined to her private gallery and the Art Institute. She was also a vital supporter of the city's Hull House, the paradigm of social welfare programming in early twentieth-century America. Hull House was founded in 1889 by Jane Addams and Ellen Gates Starr to serve as a social services center in the predominantly immigrant near west side neighborhood of Halsted and Polk streets (now part of the University of Illinois at Chicago's campus). Addams believed that art and culture could enhance the quality of life for the community's poor, and she began organizing art classes as part of the settlement house's broad programs to elevate their difficult living circumstances. By 1891, she had built the Butler Art Gallery, the first of Hull House's twelve satellite buildings, to exhibit works of art on loan from wealthy Chicago families. The immigrant population of the city was increasing markedly, and the Mexican community was centered not far from the house. The Hull House Kilns, a commercial pottery operation run by the institution, became one of the most important ties between the settlement house and the local Mexican community, allowing immigrant craftspeople to engage in their ceramic traditions.

Through her renown in the art world, Katherine Kuh was able to persuade artists to teach at Hull House, sometimes for free. Chicago artists such as Morris Topschevsky, Julio de Diego, and Charles White, all of whom traveled to Mexico to work with the Taller, also taught at the house. They brought back to the Chicago cultural community a new source of inspiration for those looking to share in a socially and politically engaged art. In 1925, Jane Addams herself went to Mexico. As a social reformer, she was drawn to the political agenda of the art she saw there. She met with Eulalia Guzmán, one of José Vasconcelos's edu-

cators, as well as other members of the Ministerio de Educación in Mexico City. Addams intended to acquire and share with her home city an understanding of the cultural landscape of Mexico. She invited Mexican artists to teach at Hull House, while art teachers from her center traveled to Mexico in exchange. For several months in 1936, Mexican photographer Manuel Alvarez Bravo taught at Hull House, further fueling the interest in and sympathy with Mexican peoples and their culture.[12]

The cross-cultural link established by Jane Addams and others at Hull House made Chicago an important center of cultural exchange with Mexican artists. In time, the WPA, which had been a critical source of funding, terminated its financial support of programs at the settlement house. However, Katherine Kuh continued to use her formidable influence to convince artists to teach there *pro bono*. Soon, several art programs at Hull House, especially fresco painting, rivaled those offered at the Art Institute of Chicago.

Eleanor Coen and Pablo O'Higgins stand in front of a mural by Diego Rivera in Mexico. *Photo courtesy of Noah and Katie Kahn.*

Eleanor Coen (Coney) (1916-)

Eleanor Coen and her husband Max Kahn were at the forefront of the Chicago art scene in the 1940s and '50s, as well as leaders in the city's involvement with the TGP. Coney, as she liked to be called, met Max Kahn at the School of the Art Institute of Chicago (SAIC), where she took lithography classes under his direction. She also studied painting with Boris Anisfeld and printmaking with Francis Chapin, later becoming Chapin's assistant. Both Coney and Kahn were involved in the WPA's Federal Art Project in Chicago from 1939 to 1940. This program, which hired artists to provide art for government buildings and to document the harsh economic conditions of the time, was a great opportunity for the two to develop their skills and styles, since they were under no pressure to sell their work (plate 37).

In 1941, Coney became the first woman to win the James Nelson Raymond Traveling Fellowship, which was awarded to the Art Institute student with the best work. She chose to study in Mexico, even though recipients of the fellowship traditionally studied in Europe. Coney and Kahn made the decision to go to Mexico primarily to avoid the inhospitable atmosphere of Europe during World War II. Mexico was a logical choice for the pair because of their support of leftist political movements. In addition, a growing number of their fellow Chicago artists were traveling to Mexico during the 1930s and '40s.

They drove to Mexico with Julio de Diego, another artist from the city, in a Ford Runabout with a rumble seat, where Kahn sat (Coney loved to drive).[13] Leaving the car at the border, they quickly inserted themselves into the Mexican lifestyle and political culture while living with Alfredo Zalce, their closest friend in Mexico City. The couple also became friends with Leopoldo Méndez, Pablo O'Higgins, and Angel Bracho. Coen and Kahn soon became active members of the TGP and encouraged other Chicagoans, including Morris "Toppy" Topchevsky and his brother "Top," to follow. Coney was in fact the first woman to work with the TGP, and it was she who influenced Mariana Yampolsky, another Chicago-area artist, to come to Mexico and join the group.

Coney and Kahn were married in 1942 after returning to Chicago, and they remained a vital part of the city's art community throughout their lives. Having studied with Francis Chapin at the SAIC, Eleanor and Max were at the vanguard of the printmaking community. In fact, in the 1940s, they mounted the first color lithography exhibition in the United States, showing their work at the Weyhe Gallery in New York City. They returned to Mexico for several summers after 1941, staying in Campeche with artist Frank Vavrushka, a former classmate of Coney's at the SAIC. The couple traveled throughout the Yucatán, painting, drawing, and visiting other TGP members.

Both Coney and Kahn created many works in Mexico City with the Taller. In addition, Kahn set up a printmaking studio in San Miguel de Allende and taught printmaking there, while Coney painted. She completed a mural on one wall of the school in San Miguel that was later damaged by building repairs and vandalism but still exits today. The school has since become a national monument. Their artistic involvement in both the United States and Mexico paved the way for other American artists to become active in the TGP, and contributed much to the strong international dimension of the workshop.

Mariana Yampolsky (1925–2002)

Mariana Yampolsky was one of those who became captivated by Chicago artists Eleanor Coen and Max Kahn's stories of working with the TGP, ultimately leaving her homeland to join the group. The daughter of a sculptor, she grew up on a 123-acre farm in Crystal Lake, outside of Chicago. At an early age, she enrolled in art classes at the Art Institute of Chicago, and by age twelve she was drawing and engraving with great skill. Her father introduced her to photography, allowing her to develop portraits he had made of the family on his camera. Mariana is best known for her powerful and deeply moving photographs of the people, customs, and cultural heritage of Mexico.

Yampolsky studied at the University of Chicago, graduating in 1944. The events of the period—the Great Depression, social turmoil, war—forever shaped her deep interest in the social and political displacement of peoples. It was in 1944 that Mariana listened entranced, as she would later describe, to a life-changing lecture by Coen and Kahn, after the couple had returned from working in Mexico City with the TGP. This lecture determined her destiny, for she too wanted to be involved with artists who were committed to social and political protest. That year, at the age of nineteen, she left for Mexico City to work with the Taller, becoming the group's first permanent female member. She also enrolled at the Escuela de Pintura y Escultura, and later took photography classes with Lola Alvarez Bravo at the Academia de San Carlos.

Later in life, Yampolsky stated that O'Higgins and Leopoldo Méndez, who was then the Taller's leader, were her chief influences. Her first works for the TGP were a series of prints for the annual May Day celebrations and a banner for a 1946 meeting of the railway workers union STFRM.[14] Both projects were important, high-profile assignments, suggesting that Yampolsky was well regarded by the workshop. During her fifteen years with the TGP (she left in 1959), she executed over sixty works, making her one of the group's ten most active members (plate 38). Yampolsky considered peasants harvesting, workers laboring in the fields, and women selling their wares—all of which she depicted in her prints—more in terms of the creative process involved in these activities than as merely quotidian chores of life. Her commitment to social issues was demonstrated in her activity for the *Mexican Ministerio de Educación*, for which she designed free textbooks for children. She also helped children learn to read and edited the *Enciclopedia infantil Colibrí*.

Yampolsky's photographs, for which she is best known, exhibit a keen, empathetic relationship with her subjects. It is interesting to note that Hannes Meyer, who became leader of the Taller upon Méndez's invitation, asked her to photograph the members of the workshop for a memorial edition of his 1949 book celebrating the group's twelfth anniversary. She continued to take photographs, curate exhibitions, design books, edit, and make prints until her death in May 2002.

Alfredo Zalce (1908–2003)

Alfredo Zalce *(see p. 28 for a more complete biography)* was perhaps the TGP artist with the strongest ties to Chicago. Zalce was married to Chicago painter Frances du Casse, and he spent much time in the city teaching, exhibiting, and working with other area artists. He acquired his first press roller in Chicago and brought it back to Mexico, where he had a whole press built around it.[15] In 1934, the Italian Court in Chicago held an exhibition of his drawings and watercolors, which received an enthusiastic response. Also in 1934, Zalce became a member of

detail of plate 31

the Associated American Artists. Gerta Katz recalls that Zalce had close relationships with other Chicago artists. Several of his prints in this exhibition came directly from Samuel and Gerta Katz's collection and Max Kahn and Eleanor Coen's collection of works by their TGP colleagues.

Elizabeth Catlett (1919–)

Of the women artists associated with the TGP, probably the best known to American audiences is African-American printmaker and sculptor Elizabeth Catlett. Born about 1919 in Washington DC, Catlett was married briefly to Chicago artist Charles White. The two met in 1941 while Catlett was working in the city with friend Margaret Goss Burroughs, one of the founders of the Chicago South Side Community Center, a vital hub for African-American artists and writers. Catlett had won first prize at the American Negro Exposition in Chicago in 1940 for a sculpture of a mother and child. In 1946, she received a Julius Rosenwald Fellowship that allowed her and Charles White to travel to Mexico to work with the TGP. Their marriage did not last long, and by 1947 she was married to Taller artist Francisco Mora, after which she often referred to herself as Betsy Mora. Both Catlett and Mora worked in Mexico with the TGP until 1966.

Even before she arrived in Mexico, Elizabeth Catlett was deeply involved in political activism. She moved there at the height of McCarthyism, and had she stayed in the United States, she would have been targeted for her leftist political views. Already an established artist, Catlett was immediately asked to collaborate on several important Taller initiatives, including the national literacy project and, later, Vincente Lombardo Toledano's 1952 presidential election campaign and the 1960 series *450 Años de Lucha: Homenaje al Pueblo Mexicano* (450 Years of Struggle: Homage to the Mexican People). In 1946, she created a series of linocuts entitled The Negro Woman, which depict, in her words, the inner strength and dignity of black women. The TGP's *Estampas de la Revolución Mexicana*, produced at the same time, influenced this series. As she became increasingly immersed in the political ideology of the Taller's mission, Catlett began to change her style to parallel that of the workshop's artists. Her once boldly angular figures gave way to more rounded, textured forms. The subtle tonal ranges and agile carving she achieved in lithography matched the level of her most accomplished colleagues.

A permanent member of the Taller from 1949 onward, Catlett believed that her art could make a contribution to the political and social struggle of Mexican women. Early on in her career, she had identified with the struggles of minority peoples and the victims of social and political oppression (plate 39). In 1970, she was quoted in *Ebony* magazine as saying, "My work speaks for both my peoples," commenting on her concern for the injustices suffered by both her African-American and her adopted Mexican sisters. Images of strong women form the central theme of her work, and though she was deeply committed to the artistic ideals of the TGP and to her adopted country of Mexico, where she lived for thirty years, she never lost her connection to her African-American identity, continuing to create works that celebrated the black woman throughout her career.

4. BRIEF BIOGRAPHIES OF ADDITIONAL ARTISTS IN THE EXHIBITION

Alberto Beltrán (1923–2002)

Alberto Beltrán grew up working in his father's tailoring shop. As a teenager, he enrolled in night classes in graphic art at the Academia de San Carlos and the Academia de Gráfica Libre. His training in commercial graphics is reflected in the extremely visually communicative style of his work. While struggling to find a job, Beltrán briefly illustrated comic strips for a Mexican newspaper. In 1944, he joined the TGP and became involved in literacy campaigns, publishing flyers for a program through the Instituto Indigenista. Beltrán was also a founding member of both the Instituto de Bellas Artes and the Academia de San Carlos. After his retirement from the TGP, he became an editor at various liberal Mexican publications, including *Ahi va el golpe* and *Coyote emplumado*. Beltrán died in 2002 in Mexico City.[16]

Angel Bracho (1911–2005)

Angel Bracho, a member of the Liga de Escritores y Artistas Revolucionarios from 1933 to 1938, was one of the first artists to join the Taller de Gráfica Popular. He participated in all of their collective expositions and collaborated in their publications. Bracho worked in a range of graphic media, especially lithography. The lithograph *Las Familias Huicholas* in this exhibition exemplifies his fluid, rhythmic style. In 1948, he became a member of the Sociedad para el Impulso de las Artes Plásticas. He published *El Rito del Sol de la Tribu de los Huichols*, an album of four lithographs, for the TGP in 1940. His close relationship with leading mural painters led him to collaborate with Alfredo Zalce and others.

Arturo García Bustos (1926–)

A student of Frida Kahlo (these students became known as "*los Fridos*"), Bustos's early studies were in painting. Later he also worked as a printmaker and muralist. With his wife Rina Lazo, primary assistant to Diego Rivera, they were part of the political art scene in Mexico. Bustos joined the Taller in 1945.

Arturo García Bustos is recognized as one of the greatest Mexican lithographers and as one of the best Mexican painters and muralists. His murals can be seen in the Oaxaca room of the Museum of Modern Art in Mexico, the metro station at the UNAM, and the stairways of the Municipal Palace in Oaxaca, to mention only a few. Bustos's works center on social and political criticism and protest against injustice, as well as a constant fight for peace. Currently, Bustos lectures on Mexican art and is currently working on a new mural project.

Francisco Dosamantes (1911–1986)

Francisco Dosamantes was a member of the LEAR before joining the TGP in 1937. Prior to working with the Taller, he studied at the Academia de San Carlos and, in 1928, was a part of the painters' organization Treinta-treinta. Throughout his career, Dosamantes was active as a teacher, working in Mexico City high schools until 1940 and serving as the general secretary of the Unión de los Profesores de Artes Plásticos in 1941. From 1941 to 1945, like other TGP members, he dedicated himself to participating in cultural missions and teaching in rural schools. He painted several murals during his travels and acted as director at the school of painting in Campeche in the Yucatán peninsula. Dosamantes was also devoted to promoting literacy, a goal he advanced by illustrating books for the Ministerio de la Enseñanza Pública.[17]

Heavy modeling and a sharp graphic quality characterize Dosamantes's prints. In his work with the TGP, he often depicted scenes of the indigenous peoples of Mexico and figures with an overt antifascist sentiment. His prints of rural communities particularly reveal the political attitude shared by members of the Taller, upholding these collective societies as examples of functioning Communism. Dosamantes used his bold, clear style to produce grand-scale promotional posters for the Taller de Gráfica Popular's exhibitions.

Jesús Escobedo (1918–1978)

Jesús Escobedo was born in the small Mexican town of El Oro but moved to Mexico City with his family. He began his painting education at the Santiago Rebull Centro Popular de la Pintura, and from 1935 to 1937 he was part of the LEAR, for whom he created antifascist posters. In July 1945, he became a member of the TGP. Also in 1945, he received a scholarship from the Guggenheim Foundation to live in New York State and work on a mural project for a school in Lexington. Escobedo's work especially emphasizes large cities (such as Mexico City and New York City) and the idea that the individual is often sacrificed in favor of the industrial and modern. He has been included in several exhibitions in the United States, including at the Art Institute of Chicago.

Andrea Gómez (1926–)

Though she was born in Mexico City, Andrea Gómez soon moved with her family to Morelia, Michoacán. It was in Morelia that Gómez's grandmother, the famous revolutionary author Juana B. Gutiérrez de Mendoza, encouraged her to pursue art. In 1940, Gómez returned to Mexico City to study at the Academia de San Carlos. There, she met Mariana Yampolsky, who urged her to join the TGP. Gómez, though, would not join the group until 1949, after marrying TGP artist Alberto Beltrán. Between 1940 and 1949, she worked as a commercial artist at various advertising firms. She was commissioned to make illustrations for organizations such as the Instituto Indígena Nacional and the Secretaría para la Enseñanza Pública. During her time as a member of the TGP from 1949 to 1960, Gómez focused mainly on creating pamphlets and posters for political rallies, union meetings, and antinuclear protests. Although it was rare for a female member of the TGP to contribute so heavily to prints for political campaigns, Gómez transferred her experience from advertising into these political works. In 1956, she won the Premio Nacional de Grabado for her print *La Niña de la Basura*. She also founded the Casa de Cultura del Pueblo and the Taller de Dibujo Infantil Arco Iris, two art centers in Mexico. Currently, Gómez is focusing on portraiture and studies of Flemish painting.

Jules Heller (1919–2008)

An important printmaker and beloved teacher, Jules Heller was born in the Bronx and raised in Brooklyn. He first studied printmaking while attending Townsend Harris High School in Flushing, New York. After receiving a bachelor's degree from Arizona State University, a master's degree from Columbia University, and a doctorate from the University of Southern California, and serving five years as an instructor in the Army Air Forces during World War II, Heller pursued a career in collegiate education. Visiting professorships took him to Thailand and Argentina, and he later served as head of the Fine Arts Department at the University of Southern California. He went on to become the founding dean of the College of Arts and Architecture at Penn State University (1963–68), dean of the Faculty of Fine Arts at York University in Toronto (1968–73), and finally dean of the College of Fine Arts at Arizona State (1976–85), before retiring in Scottsdale, Arizona. Besides teaching, Heller also wrote several textbooks that have remained a standard for the classroom, including *Printmaking Today* (1958). He received numerous prestigious honors and awards, including the Fulbright Fellowship, for his contributions to printmaking and art education, before he died of cancer in January 2008. The print room at Arizona State University, Tempe, is named after him.

Throughout his career, Heller took a particular interest in Mexican printmaking, especially the works of Leopoldo Méndez. In 1947, he and his wife honeymooned in Mexico and worked at the TGP as visiting artists. This was just the first of many trips Heller made there. He spent significant time in Méndez's studio, studying his works extensively and eventually writing his biography. "Before I ever met him, I was well aware of his powerful linocuts and lithographs," noted Heller in the memoir. His study on Méndez was the first attempt to catalog the artist's work and to distinguish him from other Mexican printmakers. Through his contributions to the TGP and his attentive biography of its founder, Heller helped to immortalize this significant moment in the history of Mexican art.[18]

Elena Huerta (1908–1997)

Elena Huerta was born in Saltillo, Coahuila, Mexico, and was the first of four Mexican-born women to join the TGP. She began her studies in 1921 at the Academia de Pintura de Saltillo, under the instruction of Rubén Herrera. Upon moving to Mexico City in 1927, she enrolled at the Academia de San Carlos, where she took drawing, painting, and printmaking classes with Carlos Mérida for the next three years. In 1929, she also taught art classes at the Secretaría de la Enseñanza Pública. Huerta was a founding member of the LEAR in 1933. Along with several other artists, including Leopoldo Méndez, she began the first puppet theater group in Mexico. Huerta traveled extensively both before and during her involvement with the TGP; she lived and worked in the former Soviet Union from 1941 to 1946 and visited China and Cuba in the late 1950s, participating in numerous exhibitions.

Although Huerta was first invited to the TGP in 1939, she did not become a permanent member until 1948. She remained active in the group until 1953, meanwhile serving as the director of the José Guadalupe Posada and José Clemente Orozco galleries in Mexico City. Outside of her involvement with the Taller, Huerta also produced independent work, including a mural in her hometown of Saltillo. She devoted some of her time to illustrating books, and in 1960 she published a book of her illustrations on rural Mexican women.[19] Huerta was the first director of the Galería José María Velasco (founded in 1951 by the Insituto Nacional de Bellas Artes), where she sought to promote the dissemination of Mexican culture.

detail of plate 35

Leopoldo Méndez (1902–1969)

The son of a shoemaker, Leopoldo Méndez is considered the principal founder and leader of the Taller de Gráfica Popular. He was also an important painter, muralist, and teacher. Highly regarded during his lifetime, he won many honors and prizes and was given important exhibitions of his work early in his career. Méndez is known for prints depicting the atrocities of war, the hardships of the *campesinos* (peasants), warnings of the threat of international fascist factions, and satires of governmental corruption, as seen in plate 20. His works were published and exhibited internationally, bringing him and his colleagues worldwide recognition. In 1939 he received a Guggenheim grant, and in 1946 he won the First National Prize for Graphic Art in Mexico. Méndez illustrated the book *Incidentes melódicos del mundo irracional* (an edition of which is in the Snite's Hayes Collection) in 1944, and in 1947 he created ten engravings used for the movie *Río escondido* (many of these engravings are also part of the Museum's holdings). One hundred forty of his prints, including plate 36, were exhibited in 1945 by the Art Institute of Chicago.

Méndez was responsible for the survival of the TGP well into the 1940s. With the end of the presidency of Lázaro Cárdenas in 1940, the Taller's production of strictly political prints decreased somewhat, and the group turned to more commercial work such as books and folios. The workshop became a vital center for collaboration, with artists from all over the world coming to Mexico City to work. Opportunities to participate in creative collaborative projects with guest artists shifted the Taller's artistic focus toward broader subject matter, attracting the support of patrons in the United States. But as the artists moved from prints that addressed Mexican social issues to images that celebrated the history and society of the indigenous peoples and works that supported or condemned world politics, the group lost some of its popularity toward the end of the 1940s. Plates 25 and 26 illustrate Méndez's shifting focus.

Many members resigned during this time, but under Méndez's influence the remaining artists adapted their images to Mexico's changing political landscape. Around 1942, the Swiss architect Hannes Meyer became the Taller's business manager and established a publishing house for the workshop called La Estampa Mexicana. His leadership came at a decisive point in the TGP's history, as the group was beginning to struggle both financially and ideologically. He remained with the Taller until his return to Switzerland in 1949, but Méndez was always the group's spiritual and philosophical leader.

Adolfo Mexiac (1927–)

Adolfo Mexiac was the son of peasants. His humble upbringing greatly influenced his work, which has been recognized throughout the world for its imagery of friendship. He was able to channel his everyday childhood experiences into portrayals of rural life, often depicting working class people with social, political, and economic themes (plate 27). Mexiac trained at the Escuela de Bellas Artes de Morelia and then, upon moving to Mexico City, at the Academia de San Carlos. He also spent time learning the medium of graphic arts at the Escuela de Artes la Esmeralda. It was there that he studied under Leopoldo Méndez and Pablo O'Higgins, who—along with Posada and Chavez Morado—were some of his main artistic influences.

Mexiac is internationally recognized, showing in countries as wide-ranging as Mexico, Poland, the Czech Republic, Japan, Italy, Puerto Rico, Germany, and the United States. He is best known as an engraver and is especially revered for his xylography skills. In addition, he is skilled in mediums such as woodcut, color woodblock, illustration, and mural painting. Mexiac became a member of the Academia de Artes del Salón de la Plástica Mexicana in 1956 and showed frequently with the Taller de Gráfica Popular. He received an award of merit from Bulgaria and the Czech Republic for his promotion of friendship through his art.

Francisco Mora (1922–2002)

Francisco Mora was married to another artist associated with the TGP, Elizabeth Catlett. Their marriage lasted over fifty years, during which time they collaborated on many projects. Catlett notes that it was Mora's willingness to share in their professional artistic careers, as well as their home duties, that allowed her to work as prolifically as she did. Mora joined the TGP in 1941, and in 1947 he published a series of lithographs depicting the life of the miner. He also created award-winning prints as part of the Mexican government's campaign for literacy. Mora's involvement with the TGP included illustrating books, making posters for trade unions, and creating prints for magazines and newspapers.[20]

Isidoro Ocampo (1910–1983)

Isidoro Ocampo was born in Veracruz and moved to Mexico City as a child. At the age of eighteen, he began four years of study at the Academia de San Carlos. Before joining the Taller de Gráfica Popular in 1937, Ocampo was a member of the LEAR and worked for the Ministerio de Educación as a professor of the plastic arts in Mexico City.[21]

Pablo O'Higgins (1904–1983)

Another founding member of the Taller de Gráfica Popular, Pablo O'Higgins, an American by birth, connected the TGP to the American art scene and dedicated himself to depicting the Mexican working class. Born in Salt Lake City, O'Higgins was dissatisfied with academic, institutional methods; his desire to work in a communal setting led him to continue his art education in Mexico. In 1924, he arrived there to work with Diego Rivera. For several years, O'Higgins worked as Rivera's assistant, learning from him the techniques of mural painting. He left Mexico in the early 1930s to spend a formative year in the Soviet Union, cementing his commitment to defending the rights of the working class.[22]

O'Higgins established himself as a significant member of the art community in Mexico, and in 1929 he met and collaborated with Leopoldo Méndez.[23] After forming a friendship, the two artists, along with Alfredo Zalce, founded the Liga de Escritores y Artistas Revolucionarios in 1934. Upon the dissolution of the LEAR in 1937, O'Higgins and Méndez continued their artistic collaboration with the formation of the Taller de Gráfica Popular in Mexico City. O'Higgins brought the expressive style of his mural work to the prints he contributed to the TGP. Working mostly in the lithographic medium, he developed a distinctive oeuvre. A loose, undulating line characterizes his work, in contrast to the typically more angular, graphic line of other TGP members. O'Higgins's prints often depict quotidian scenes of Mexican workers, reflecting the artist's *obrerismo*, or compassion for the struggle of the manual laborer (plate 29). He does not imbue these figures with an overtly propagandistic attitude but rather with a sympathetic, dignified character.

While living in Mexico and working with the TGP, O'Higgins retained ties to the country of his birth. He continued to exhibit his paintings and prints in the United States and received mural commissions in San Francisco and Seattle.[24] Notably, he created an invaluable association between the Taller and artists in the United States. Through O'Higgins, the workshop was able to arrange exhibitions in the States, increasing American recognition of the Mexican art scene.

Fernando Castro Pacheco (1918–)

Fernando Castro Pacheco was born in Mérida, Yucatán. He began his formal artistic training in 1933 at the Mérida Escuela de Bellas Arte, where he learned the skills of engraving and painting. In 1941, he cofounded the Escuela Libre de Las Artes Plásticas de Yucatán. His lithographs and paintings were first exhibited at the Galería de la Universidad de Yucatán in 1942.

Pacheco initially painted wall murals around the city of Mérida, but in 1943 he moved to Mexico City and became associated with the Taller de Gráfica Popular. His work with the TGP reflected his support for union workers and the lower class, often portraying the poor and suffering in Mexico. When his portfolio was first shown in the Taller's 1942 exhibition in Mexico City, Pacheco gained international attention. He exhibited his work in San Francisco in 1945 and in Havana in 1947.

Returning to Mexico City in 1949, Pacheco was named a professor of the Escuela National de Partes Plásticas. In 1963, the Institución Nacional de Bellas Artes commissioned him to travel and study the artistic styles in Spain, Italy, France, England, Holland, and Belgium. He moved back to Mérida in 1973 and completed his murals for the governor's palace, depicting life in the Yucatán after Spanish control.

Alfredo Zalce (1908–2003)

Alfredo Zalce enrolled in the Academia de San Carlos in 1924, launching his multifaceted career. Continuing his studies at the Escuela de Talla Directa in 1931, he concentrated on lithography with Carlos Mérida. He also worked as an instructor of art, in 1930 founding the Escuela de Pintura y Escultura in Taxco, Guerrero.[25] In 1934, Zalce established the Liga de Escritores y Artistas Revolucionarios with Leopoldo Méndez and Pablo O'Higgins. As a member of the LEAR collective, he acted as a liaison to provincial artists and rural teachers. Beginning in 1932, he had been traveling throughout Mexico with the Profesores Itinerantes Institutos Federales as an instructor of art.[26] During this time, Zalce dedicated himself not only to teaching but also to working in mural decoration and immersing himself in the culture of the rural working class. He traveled in 1945 to the Yucatán, Campeche, and Quintana Roo.[27] Living in these areas, he developed an understanding and compassion for the social struggles of such communities that would characterize his work in the 1940s. Notably, he published a series of eight lithographs with the TGP, the *Estampas de Yucatán*, depicting everyday scenes of rural life.

In 1937, Alfredo Zalce, along with Leopoldo Méndez, Pablo O'Higgins, Luis Arenal, and Angel Bracho, dissolved the LEAR and founded the Taller de Gráfica Popular. Zalce's striking lithograph and linocut work furthered the political agenda of the TGP on both a domestic and an international front. His oversized, bold propagandistic posters best describe his contribution to the group's political intentions (plate 32). Zalce used straightforward iconography to catch the eye of the viewer and quickly convey a concept. The figures represented in his posters are especially marked by a sense of heroism, and his prints act as emphatic statements designed to promulgate a proletarian identity.[28]

Zalce's smaller lithographs, often characterized by cartoon-like caricatures, were also intended to disseminate information to the Mexican public and advance the TGP's point of view. Much of Zalce's work for the Taller is marked by a sense of turbid, dark comedy. This is especially evident in *La Prensa al Servicio del Imperialismo* (plate 31) and *México se Transforma en una Gran Ciudad* (plate 18), in which Zalce has distorted the physiognomy of his figures to create morose, chaotic compositions. In his significant work for the 1947 collective folio *Estampas de la Revolución Mexicana*, Zalce depicts anti-Cárdenas politicians through sordid, vilifying caricatures (plates 33, 34).

Zalce exhibited his prints independently both in Mexico and abroad and took part in all collective exhibitions of the TGP. He was especially praised during the exhibition of Mexican art at the Italian Court in Chicago. Due to political differences, Zalce left the Taller in 1947, shortly before the group's informal dissolution. He subsequently worked in a wide variety of media, including sculpture, ceramics, jewelry, watercolor, mural painting, and printing. About a year before his death in January 2003, Alfredo Zalce's contribution to Mexican culture was acknowledged with the National Art Award.

detail of plate 32

The Plates of the Exhibition

PLATE 1

Los Tranviarios Luchan en Beneficio de Todo el Pueblo, 1942 Wallstreet, 10 Centavos Más por Hora, Wall Street! (Monopolio, Algunos Tragan Mucho y Tragamonedas) y 4000 Horgares sin Pan en: Los Tranviarios Luchan en Beneficio de Todo el Pueblo, Mexico

The Railroaders Fight for the Benefit of the People, 1942 Wall Street, 10 Cents More per Hour, Wall Street! (Monopoly, Some Swallow a Lot and Slot Machine) and 4000 Homes without Bread: The Railroaders Fight for the Benefit of the People, Mexico

1943

Leopoldo Méndez Mexican, 1902–1969

Linocut, 25.25 x 34.25 inches (64.1 x 87 cm)

Gift of Charles S. Hayes '65

2009.008.007

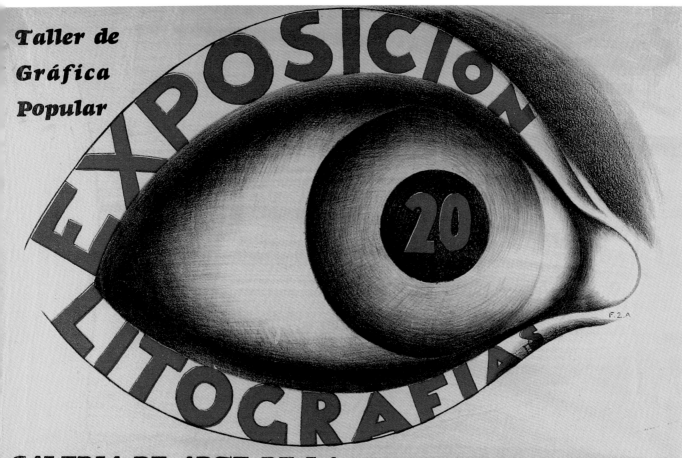

PLATE 2
Taller de Gráfica Popular. Exposición 20 Litografías.
Galería de Arte de la Universidad Nacional
Taller de Gráfica Popular. Exhibition 20 Lithographs.
Galeria de Arte de la Universidad Nacional
1939
Francisco Dosamantes, Mexican, 1911–1986
Lithograph, 16.25 x 22.19 inches (41.3 x 56.35 cm)
Gift of Charles S. Hayes '65
2009.012.031

This early, large-scale poster publicizing a 1939 Taller de Gráfica Popular print exhibition epitomizes the graphic modeling and acute line characteristic of TGP work. Francisco Dosamantes's image of an abstract eye, printed in red and black, dominates the composition. The poster is simple, designed to be prominent and to catch the attention of passersby. The date and location of the exhibition appear in alternating red and black ink, increasing the legibility of the notice. In his bold manner, Dosamantes has added the words *exposicíon litografías* to the lids of the striking eye, in tiny yet prominent red letters. The number *20* pierces the center of the pupil.

PLATE 3

Vida y Drama de México. 20 Años de Vida del Taller de Gráfica Popular . . . Palacio de Bellas Artes . . . del 19 de noviembre al 28 de diciembre

Life and Drama of Mexico. 20 Years of the Taller de Gráfica Popular . . . Palacio de Bellas Artes . . . From November 19 to December 28

1957

Alberto Beltrán, Mexican, 1923–2002

Two-color linocut, 25.5 x 16.56 inches (64.77 x 42.1 cm)

Gift of Charles S. Hayes '65

2009.012.001

This 1957 print commemorates the twentieth anniversary of the TGP, announcing an exhibition of various TGP artists' works in Mexico City's Palacio de Bellas Artes. In the center of the poster, Alberto Beltrán depicts the hands of a TGP artist carving a linocut of a man seemingly brought to life as he rises from the printing plate. In the background, a wealthy *calavera* (living skeleton) drinks wine on the right, while on the left a peasant turns his head away from the calavera's scandalous ways. Beltrán's print serves as a social commentary on postrevolutionary Mexico, revealing the disparities that still existed among the various social classes.[29]

PLATE 4
El Fascismo. 7a. Conferencia. El Fascismo Japones
Fascism. 7th Conference. Japanese Fascism
1939
Isidoro Ocampo, Mexican, 1910–1983
Lithograph in two colors 17.13 x 23.15 inches (43.5 x 58.8 cm)
Gift of Charles S. Hayes '65
2009.012.006

Among the Taller de Gráfica Popular's earliest projects was a collaboration with the Liga Pro-Cultura Alemana, a vehemently antifascist group of expatriate Germans.[30] As one of its initiatives, the Liga held a public lecture series in Mexico City addressing the threat of fascism. The TGP created a set of eighteen large-scale poster prints to advertise the lectures.[31] In his 1939 poster publicizing the conference, Isidoro Ocampo depicted Japanese emperor Hirohito as a menacing spider overtaking Chinese territory.

Japan had been invading China since 1931. On November 11, 1937, its military assaults escalated to a bloody massacre in the Chinese capital city of Nanjing. Often referred to as the Rape of Nanjing, this massacre, during which Japanese soldiers held mass executions and looted the city, lasted for six weeks and wiped out an estimated 250,000 to 300,000 people.[32] The caricature of Hirohito as a black widow consuming China alludes to this slaughter, which would have been addressed at the Liga's conference. Ocampo uses his print to vilify Hirohito, portraying him to the Mexican public as synonymous with the evils of fascism.

¡VICTORIA!

Los artistas del Taller de Gráfica Popular nos unimos al júbilo de todos los trabajadores y hombres progresistas de México y del Mundo por el triunfo del glorioso Ejército Rojo y de las armas de todas las Naciones Unidas sobre la Alemania Nazi, como el paso más trascendente para la

DESTRUCCION TOTAL DEL FASCISMO

PLATE 5, *opposite*
Victoria
Victory
1945
Angel Bracho Mexican, 1911–2005
Linocut, 29.13 x 20.75 inches (73.98 x 52.76 cm)
Gift of Charles S. Hayes '65
2009.012.021

PLATE 6
El Fascismo. 8a. Conferencia
Fascism. 8th Conference
1939
Jesús Escobedo, Mexican, 1918–1978
Lithograph, 17 x 23.75 inches (43.2 x 60.3 cm)
Gift of Charles S. Hayes '65
2009.012.022

LAZARO CARDENAS, ilustre ex-presidente de México, hombre del pueblo y símbolo de sus mejores luchas. Por sus labios, la patria ha expresado sus más claros y rotundos anhelos de libertad y justicia social, amistad, comprensión y paz para todos los pueblos. El eco internacional de su invariable actitud pacifista ha conquistado, para él y para México simpatía, prestigio y respetabilidad. Este gran mexicano ha sido distinguido con el Premio Stalin de la Paz. Unámonos todos en el justo homenaje que los hombres de cinco continentes le rinden por su ejemplar actitud.

FIEL A LAS MEJORES banderas revolucionarias, LAZARO CARDENAS supo encauzar por canales de beneficio popular los recursos de la nación. En Zacatepec, donde aún se escucha el grito de Zapata, así como en tantos otros rincones del país, sacudido por la heroica lucha de nuestros campesinos, Cárdenas puso el poder al servicio de los sectores mayoritarios de nuestra población. Tierra y libertad, para que el campesino encuentre en el trabajo su liberación y no su esclavitud. ¡Honremos al mexicano ilustre!

HOMENAJE A CARDENAS
DOMINGO 26 DE FEBRERO A LAS 10 HORAS

Su reconocida convicción pacifista, que dió jerarquía al nombre de la patria en el mundo entero, lo hace hoy objeto de una distinción mundial: el Premio Stalin de la Paz. Cárdenas representa hoy a los hombres que, en todo el mundo, están luchando por la paz y por el entendimiento entre los pueblos. ¡Unámonos al homenaje del mundo pacifista a Cárdenas.

EN LA CHOZA MAS HUMILDE de nuestro país, hay siempre un lugar de veneración para LAZARO CARDENAS. Alejado de las urgencias y responsabilidades de la vida pública, Cárdenas sigue haciendo honor a su historia y su voz es siempre un llamado a la paz, a la concordia, a la tolerancia, en un mundo amenazado por la guerra. Hoy, el nombre de Cárdenas es pronunciado con respeto y simpatía. Su designación como acreedor al Premio Stalin de la Paz, es el reconocimiento de su limpia y leal militancia por la paz para todos, sin tolerancias.

NUEVO TEATRO IDEAL — SERAPIO RENDON 15
Movimiento Mexicano por la Paz

Andrea Gómez's print *Tributo a Cárdenas* (plate 7) demonstrates the respect and admiration the Mexican people felt toward their former president. This poster advertises a meeting to honor Cárdenas for his selection as a recipient of the Stalin Peace Prize. Created in 1949 by the Soviet government, the peace prize was awarded annually to an individual who "strengthened peace among peoples."[33]

Each of the four images of Cárdenas's presidency in this print features a scene and a text glorifying him for his achievements. The passage under the stoic profile portrait at the top left states that Cárdenas had "expressed its [Mexico's] most clear and resounding desires for liberty and social justice, friendship, understanding and peace for all the people." To the right of this portrait is a scene of Cárdenas overseeing the construction of a factory. In the third image, he is monumentalized, placed in the front corner overlooking a landscape so that he appears much larger than the rest of the figures. The writing accompanying this picture exalts Cárdenas for his loyalty to the Mexican people and for his commitment to "land and liberty, so that the peasant finds through his work his liberation and not his slavery." Cárdenas's arm sweeps over the landscape as he leads Mexico to a better future. The scene highlights many of the reforms Cárdenas enacted: the plow and oxen represent his agrarian reform, while the factories expelling steam symbolize his effort to improve labor conditions. The last image depicts a peasant family tacking a picture of Cárdenas on the wall of their hut; as the text below reads, "In the most humble shack of our country, there is always a place of worship for Lázaro Cárdenas."

PLATE 9
Paremos la Agracion hacia la Clase Trabajadora!
Let Us Stop the Aggression toward the Working Class!
1950
Leopoldo Méndez, Mexican, 1902–69
Linocut, 26 x 34.88 inches (66.04 x 88.6 cm)
Gift of Charles S. Hayes '65
2009.012.009

In this poster, Méndez endorses the 1950 and 1951 miners' strikes against the American Smelting and Refining Company in Palau, Nueva Rosita, and Cloete.[34] Small text at the bottom of the print urges the viewer to aid the miners in their struggle by sending donations to the union. Méndez presents a heroic depiction of a miner, identifiable by his helmet and mask, extending his arm to defend the woman and child behind him from a threatening bayonet. In his right hand, he grips a banner calling for a stop to "the aggression toward the working class." Through this powerful imagery, Méndez evokes an emotional response from the viewer in order to strengthen support for the miners' cause.

PLATE 10
Zapata. Toda la Tierra para los Granjeros
Zapata. All the Land for the Farmers
Date unknown
Unidentified artist
Linocut, 11.75 x 8 inches (29.85 x 20.3 cm)
Gift of Charles S. Hayes '65
2009.008.018

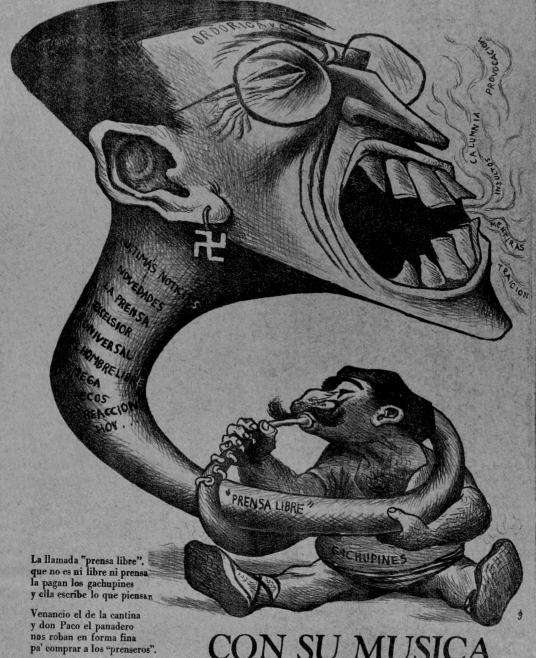

The artists of the TGP led many initiatives in support of antifascist causes in Europe.[35] Produced in 1939, toward the end of the Spanish Civil War, this print contains a strong antifascist overtone.[36] The image, (plate 11), which has been attributed to both Isidoro Ocampo and José Chávez Morado, was printed in a popular serial in Mexican newspapers called the "*Risa del Pueblo*" (Laughter of the People), which often included political cartoons similar to this one.[37] The artist is satirizing the notion of the free press in Mexico and denouncing Mexican journalists and newspapers with pro-Franco inclinations. Sprawled clumsily on the floor is a foul *gachupine* (an insulting nickname for Spaniards), whose feet are emanating a strong stench. The *gachupine* has manipulated the body of newspaper editor Miguel Ordorica into a horn, upon whose neck various names of pro-Franco Mexican newspapers have been etched.[38] Fitted with a swastika earring, Ordorica is exposing the crimes that he and other pro-Franco newspapers have committed against the Mexican people, as the *gachupine* blows words such as *calumnia* (defamation) and *mentiras* (lies) out of his mouth. Located lower on the neck of Ordorica are the words *prensa libre* (free press); the artist ridicules this notion by showing how easily the Mexican press can be manipulated by the *gachupines*.

Underneath the *gachupine* and Ordorica, on the lower left, is a poem lamenting the state of the Mexican press. The poem tells the audience that "the name 'free press' / which is neither free nor press / is paid by the *gachupines* / so they can write what they think." Later, in the second stanza, it asserts that the pro-Franco Mexicans have "robbed us in fine form." To the right of these verses, more text assures the viewer that the horn's music is only for the "other side," not for the Mexicans who oppose Franco. While it may have claimed to be free, the press had become, according to the TGP, a malleable horn used by the Franco sympathizers to spread their fascist beliefs.

Alfredo Zalce's poster the *Risa del Pueblo* (plate 12) also takes on the aspect of a political cartoon. By juxtaposing text and image, the artist creates caricatures of contemporary political figures in order to denigrate them. Five figures—one a generic bandit and four labeled as Pablo González, Leon Ossorio, Iturbe, and Bolívar Sierra—are crowded into a gray car, the "*automóvil gris.*" They escape from a building they have raided, leaving a woman lying in the doorway.

The labeled caricatures would have resounded with the viewing public. During the revolution, Pablo González was involved in a network of thieves called the Banda del Automóvil Gris, who broke into homes by wearing police uniforms and showing fake search warrants. González was also a politician, and in 1919 he made a bid for the presidential candidacy. In order to change his image, he produced an extremely popular movie, *El automóvil gris.* This plan backfired, however, only cementing his reputation as a dishonest politician.[39] The popularity of the film would have made Zalce's reference to González as a synonym for corruption immediately apparent.

In the print, González sits at the front of the *automóvil gris*, with the late-1930s politicians Ossorio, Iturbe, and Sierra behind him. By including the anachronistic figure of González, Zalce indicts these contemporary politicians as corrupt. The three were part of the Comite de Salvación Pública, a vehemently anticommunist and anti-Cárdenas group, and thus were opposed to the political ideologies of the TGP.[40] Zalce has exaggerated their features to make them easily identifiable to the Mexican public. The stolen scroll tucked under González's arm, labeled as articles 123 and 127 of the 1917 Mexican constitution, also refers to the dishonesty of these politicians. The theft of these articles—which preserved the right to strike and prevented government officials from increasing their own salaries while in office—highlights the threat posed by these politicians.[41] At the bottom left, a poem further condemns the clownlike characters of the *automóvil gris*, denouncing the group as "not revolutionaries, nor even Mexicans." Through this distinctive, morbid comedy, Zalce has created a recognizable propagandistic image and a defense of President Cárdenas's politics.

PLATE 12, *following spread*
Risa del Pueblo
Laughter of the People
1939
Alfredo Zalce, Mexican, 1908–2003
Lithograph, 15.38 x 21.75 inches (39.05 x 55.25 cm)
Gift of Charles S. Hayes '65
2009.012.011

"LA RISA D

Una banda de rufianes
la del Automóvil Gris,
que tantos robos hizo antes
vuelve de nuevo a salir.

No son revolucionarios
ni mexicanos siquiera:
son sólo unos mercenarios
que se alquilan a cualquiera.

Don Pablo va a la cabeza
y lo sigue León Ossorio,
Iturbe y Bolívar Sierra
en ridículo jolgorio.

Son bribones chantagistas
que viven de cosas ruines,
sirviéndole a los callistas
y estafando gachupines.

L PUEBLO"

El Retorno del 'Automovil Gris'

Francisco I. Madero, Candidato Popular
Francisco I. Madero, Popular Candidate
1947
Jules Heller, American, 1919–2008
Linocut, 11.38 x 8.25 inches (29.1 x 20.96 cm)
Gift of Charles S. Hayes '65
2009.007.115.CC

Jules Heller's print *Francisco I. Madero, Candidato Popular* was made for the *Estampas de la Revolución Mexicana*. It depicts Madero as he victoriously addresses the Mexican people during his attempt to capture the presidency. Alberto Morales Jiménez's *Indice de los grabados con notas historica* states that Madero is shown traveling across the country to inform the people of his new program of government. In a propagandistic tone, he suggests that Madero, along with his vice-president José María Pino Suárez, will promote freedom and solve all of Mexico's problems.[42] The print and its accompanying explanation emphasize that Madero was elected as a result of a free and spontaneous vote.

Madero is portrayed waving to a group representative of Mexican society from a balcony. A banner to the right emblazoned with his image reads, "Partido Democrático." Heller's representation of the reformist candidate reflects the TGP's political inclinations and reinforces the ideal of a revolutionary spirit that the group sought to convey in the *Estampas*. As a tribute to the Mexican Revolution, the folio was intended to fortify the reputation of President Cárdenas, whose successors in the Partido Revolucionario Institucional (PRI) were the current ruling party.

In contrast to Heller's glorification of a revolutionary hero, Fernando Castro Pacheco's print (plate 14), also a part of the *Estampas de la Revolución Mexicana*, focuses on Victoriano Huerta, who was the dictator of Mexico from 1913 to 1914. After graduating from the Colegio Militar de Chapultepec in 1877, Huerta began his career as a military engineer. By 1902, he had ascended to the rank of brigadier general. When Francisco Madero became president in 1911, Huerta disagreed with his proposals for democracy and began planning to get rid of him. On February 18, 1913, Madero was arrested in the national palace during a military revolt, and he was murdered shortly thereafter. Huerta immediately proclaimed himself president and became a tyrannical ruler. Eventually, he was forced into exile by an uprising, and he died in 1916 of cirrhosis of the liver.[43]

Huerta is satirized in this print, depicted on a religious standard held by the oversized hand of a cleric, with a halo crowning his image. The clergyman's hand prominently displays an expensive jeweled ring, and his smiling face appears grotesque as he waves the standard of Huerta. This image of an overbearing cleric represents the ongoing power conflict between the church and state in Mexico, which was exacerbated by the creation of the 1917 constitution.[44] During this time of political turmoil, the church was attempting to gain more power, and the constitution heavily restricted its involvement in politics. Pacheco's print shows a crowd of peasants on the right behind the standard and, on the left, members of the bourgeoisie venerating Huerta's image, all with grins fixed on their faces. Through this scene, the artist satirizes not only Huerta but also the people who supported him: the church and the ignorant bourgeoisie and peasant populations.[45]

PLATE 14
Victoriano Huerta Estandarte de la Reacción
The Image of Victoriano Huerta on the Flag of Reaction
1947
Fernando Castro Pacheco, Mexican, 1918–
Linocut, 11.63 x 8.44 inches (29.53 x 21.4 cm)
Gift of Charles S. Hayes '65
2009.007.115.PP

PLATE 15
Constitución del '17
Constitution of '17
Date unknown
Elena Huerta, Mexican, 1908–1997
Linoleum cut, 12 x 16.69 inches (30.5 x 42.4 cm)
Gift of Charles S. Hayes '65
2009.007.111

In her *Constitución del '17*, Elena Huerta creates a portrait-like representation of the historical figures who contributed to the formation of the Mexican Constitution of 1917. The print does not illustrate an actual historical event but rather a fictional gathering of the constitution's supporters. These political personages are depicted in the established stereotyped form used by the Taller de Gráfica Popular in their many pamphlets, posters, and book illustrations to make the figures' identities easily recognizable to the viewer.

Venustiano Carranza, who served from 1917 to 1920 as the first president elected under the constitution, is depicted at the center of the group, presenting the new document of law. Pancho Villa, the fourth figure from the right, and Emiliano Zapata, on the far right, represent the *factionos* who, while supporting the constitution, eventually did not accept President Carranza's reforms. Indeed, Zapata would later be assassinated on Carranza's orders. The other figures in the scene represent conservative Catholics and reactionary landowners who similarly did not agree with Carranza's ideas.

PLATE 16
Asesinato del Gral. Álvaro Obregón, Dirigido por la Reacción Clerical
Assassination of Gen. Álvaro Obregón, Instigated by Clerical Reaction
1947
Fernando Castro Pacheco, Mexican, 1918–
Linocut, 8.85 x 12 inches (22.47 x 30.48 cm)
Gift of Charles S. Hayes '65
2009.007.115.LLL

As president during the height of the tension between the Mexican government and the Catholic Church, Álvaro Obregón became a target at the outbreak of the Cristero War. During this revolt, which lasted from 1926 into the 1930s, fervent Catholics banded together to fight "for Christ" and against the government.[46] Obregón became a victim of the uprising soon after he was elected president for the second time, when he was assassinated by a Cristero on July 17, 1928.[47]

This print depicts Obregón on his last day alive, while he was celebrating his reelection at a banquet in his honor. The remnants of his meal sit in front of him, as does a piece of paper on which his portrait is sketched. His assassin, José de León Toral, had presented an unfinished version of the sketch to Obregón in the restaurant. León Toral had then pretended to continue sketching next to Obregón before shooting him five times in the face.[48] Although the figure holding the pistol in the print is hidden under a sheet, the identity of the assassin is indicated by the clerical figures surrounding Obregón. After working so tirelessly to limit the power of the church, Obregón was ultimately the one made powerless, while the Cristero War continued after his death.

PLATE 17

El Gran Guerrillero Francisco Villa, 1877–1923
The Great Guerrilla Francisco Villa, 1877–1923
1947

Alberto Beltrán, Mexican, 1923–2002
Linocut, 11.875 x 8.75 inches (30.16 x 22.23 cm)
Gift of Charles S. Hayes '65
2009.007.115.KK

The TGP's heroic portrayals of revolutionaries such as Pancho Villa contributed to the promotion of Mexicanidad by celebrating Mexico's historic struggle for social equality. This print by Alberto Beltrán was included in the 1947 portfolio *Estampas de la Revolución Mexicana*. As leader of the Division of the North, one of the private revolutionary armies that fought to topple the Mexican dictator Porifirio Diaz, Villa was revered by the Mexican people as a hero.[49] His fight "for the people" parallels the TGP's goal of producing accessible art depicting the struggles of the working class. Beltrán's portrayal of Villa as a liberator is emphasized by the prominent bandolier running across his chest and by the white outline that surrounds the revolutionary and his horse, as if they were emanating light.[50] The artist achieves a strong sense of motion in the print, giving the impression that Villa's horse may take off into battle for the people at any moment.

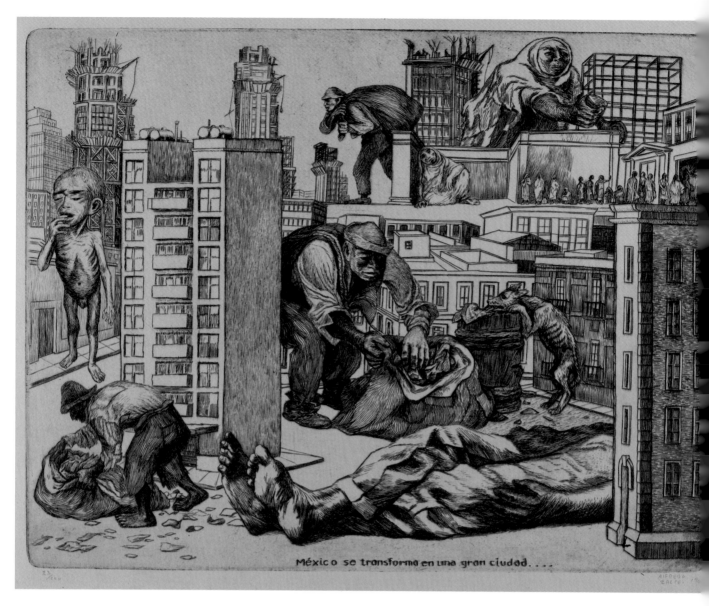

México se transforma en una gran ciudad. . . .

PLATE 18
México se Transforma en una Gran Ciudad
Mexico Transforms into a Great City
1947
Alfredo Zalce, Mexican, 1908–2003
Linocut, 12.13 x 15.5 inches (30.8 x 39.4 cm)
Gift of Charles S. Hayes '65
2009.019.018

The transformation of Mexico City was not all positive. *México se Transforma en una Gran Ciudad* reflects Alfredo Zalce's experiences in the city, where he spent most of his life. The artist created the linocut as a reaction to an autobiographical event that occurred while he was living in Mexico City's Santa Maria colony. Zalce recounts that in 1947, trash had been left to pile up on the streets while skyscrapers were being constructed. Late one night, he observed a man trying to find food in a heap of trash. When a dog came to look in the same pile, the man said, "What do you want here? Bones, meat? I don't even have food and I have to feed a family."[51] In his print, Zalce displays the man prominently, crouched over and picking through the debris with an exaggeratedly large hand, while the emaciated dog, mimicking the man's gestures, stands in the center of the composition.

The artist has created a chaotic image, where the figures—reduced to the struggle for survival—interact between towering buildings and still incomplete skyscrapers. Zalce heightens the grotesqueness by deforming the figures' physiognomies and distorting the proportion: an emaciated child stands as tall as a building, and an enormous pair of legs cuts across the composition horizontally. In this macabre pathos, Zalce articulates his regret at Mexico City's transformation into a "great city," a title that, in itself, expresses bitter irony.[52]

PLATE 19
Derecho de la Clase Obrera
The Rights of the Working Class
1951
Pablo O'Higgins, American, 1904–1983
Lithograph, 8.88 x 8.35 inches (22.54 x 21.2 cm)
Gift of Charles S. Hayes '65
2009.007.066

Members of the TGP looked to Posada's prints and appropriated the vernacular tradition that he had popularized. In *Derecho de la Clase Obrera*, Pablo O'Higgins borrows his predecessor's signature motif of the *calavera* to communicate his own message of social satire. O'Higgins may well have printed this small 1951 lithograph during the *Día de los Muertos* celebrations. His image parodies the division between the working and upper classes. A scholar and a woman, depicted as living skeletons, laugh as they dance in a frenzy; they represent education and luxury cavorting out of reach of the working class. Not only does O'Higgins quote Posada's *calaveras* but he also evokes the titles or labels that Posada often included in his prints: in the bottom left corner, he adds a scroll reading, "the rights of the working class."

O'Higgins, along with Leopoldo Méndez, was a devoted student of Posada's iconographic language. In 1930, he selected and edited a collection of prints by Posada entitled *Monografía*.[53] Other members of the workshop also regularly used the trope of the *calavera* in their prints, which often championed the working class encumbered by daily struggles. By incorporating this well-known motif from Mexican folk tradition, they could ensure that their politically motivated works would be easily read and understood by both the rural peasant and the urban working class.

PLATE 20
El Dueño de Todo
The Owner of Everything
1948
Leopoldo Méndez, Mexican, 1902–1969
Linocut, 12 x 16.31inches (30.5 x 41.43 cm)
Gift of Charles S. Hayes '65
2009.007.028

The prints by Méndez in this catalog illustrate the direct and powerful style he used to depict the social injustices faced by peasant laborers. For example, in *El Dueño de Todo*, dated to 1948, Méndez portrays a political gangster boss giving orders to a line of overburdened workers, as he rests his feet on a table, relaxing. The large, menacing figure of the owner—defined by heavy, bold, angular lines—is set in the foreground of the scene, while the workers appear as a tiny row of animals in the background. The image clearly supports the labor reforms that President Cárdenas's administration was implementing at the time. By citing the oppression of the Mexican people, Méndez levels harsh criticism at the government's former policies and the landowners.

PLATE 21
Concierto Sinfónico de Calaveras
The Symphonic Concert of Skeletons
Date unknown
Leopoldo Méndez, Mexican, 1902–1969
Relief print, 8.88 x 6.63 inches (22.54 x 16.8 cm)
Gift of Charles S. Hayes '65
2009.014.008

This image was first published as a cover for the journal *Frente a Frente* in 1934, while Méndez was still an active member of the LEAR. *Frente a Frente*, which translates as "Head to Head," was a leftist journal started by the LEAR during Cárdenas's presidency as a means of promoting art with a social message.[54] The print shown here is a somewhat later edition that appeared as part of a series of images in one of Méndez's portfolios. It is among the first examples in which Méndez recognizably employs Posada's iconography of the *calavera* to satirize the bourgeois class. In this instance, he uses the device to parody the inauguration of the Palacio de Bellas Arte in Mexico City, deriding the bourgeois excess of this historical event. Méndez depicts the muralist Diego Rivera as the *calavera* on the left and Carlos Riva Palacio, the president of the newly formed Partido Nacional Revolucionario, as the *calavera* on the right. The two men's perceived dedication to capitalist culture is illustrated by the markings of a dollar (or peso) sign and a swastika, respectively, on the backs of their chairs. The program on the floor by Rivera's foot translates to read, "Today, 'The Sun' Proletarian Series, tickets $25"; this inclusion draws attention to the inflated price of admission to the event, which was apparently intended for the middle class.

PLATE 22
El Fin del Zopilote
The End of the Vulture
1944
Leopoldo Méndez, Mexican, 1902–1969
Linocut, 7.13 x 5.5 inches (18.1 x 14 cm)
Gift of Charles S. Hayes '65
2009.007.008

El Fin del Zopilote is one of forty prints based on Yucatán folk songs that Méndez created to illustrate the 1944 book the *Incidentes melódicos del mundo irracional*. Written by Juan de la Cabada, the *Incidentes melódicos* recounts the mythical story of a snail woman, Doña Caracol, who is kidnapped by an evil vulture, El Zopilote.[55] El Zopilote holds her captive until his true nature is revealed and he meets his fate: he is hung by a rebelling crowd. This image narrates the death of El Zopilote and the liberation of Doña Caracol. El Zopilote hangs lifelessly from the branch of a bare, twisted tree, while the snail woman's saviors rejoice and dance in the glow of several bonfires.

Méndez's contribution to this book, marked by pre-Columbian imagery and a fantastic, otherworldly quality, may seem exceptional in his usually political and socially-minded oeuvre. However, he never lost sight of his Aztec and Mayan ancestry, using symbols from this fertile cultural tradition increasingly over the course of his career, especially after 1947. And even these folk images served his political message: El Zopilote has been seen to represent the oppressors of the Mexican people and leftist thought—capitalism, imperialism, and fascism.

PLATE 23
Realizado para Portada de Anna Seghers, La séptima cruz
Mexico City: El Libro Libre
Cover of Anna Seghers's, Das siebte Kreuz (The Seventh
Cross) Mexico City: El Libro Libre
1943
Leopoldo Méndez, Mexican, 1902–1969
Color relief print, 7.38 x 5.12 inches (18.73 x 13 cm)
Gift of Charles S. Hayes '65
2009.018.009

Méndez made this print, which depicts the brutality of a Nazi prison camp, for the cover of Anna Seghers's *Das siebte Kreuz (The Seventh Cross)*. Published as a Spanish-language edition in Mexico in 1943 by *El Libro Libre*, the book recounts the imprisonment of seven German socialists and their attempted escape from Nazi violence. Seghers, a German Communist and renowned author, fled Nazi oppression herself, living in exile in both Mexico and the United States.

Through *Das siebte Kreuz*, she exposed the Nazi aggression that targeted the Left in the 1930s. One of her most important works, the book was critical for revealing the realities of pre–World War II Germany to the public in the Americas.[57]

In his cover illustration, Méndez reflects the dark cruelty described by Seghers. A Nazi soldier, identifiable by his black books, uniform, and swastika armband, grabs for his gun as he disappears behind a dead tree trunk, the wood of which has been fashioned into an implement of torture for one of the seven escapees. This "seventh cross," which bears the author's name and the book title, dominates the composition through its abrupt placement in the immediate foreground. Méndez's use of bold black line and sadistic imagery replicates the sinister tone of *Das siebte Kreuz* in visual form.

PLATE 25
No Queremos la Guerra (Los Deseos de la Paz)
We Do Not Want the War (The Desires of Peace)
Date unknown
Leopoldo Méndez, Mexican, 1902–1969
Linocut, 5.75 x 8.5 inches (14.6 x 21.6 cm)
Gift of Charles S. Hayes '65
2009.007.023

PLATE 26
Resistencia
Resistance
Date unknown
Leopoldo Méndez, Mexican, 1902–1969
Linoleum cut, 11 x 14.81 inches (27.9 x 37.62 cm)
Gift of Charles S. Hayes '65
2009.007.038

The prints *No Queremos la Guerra (Los Deseos de la Paz)* (plate 25) and *Resistencia* (plate 26), which probably date from about 1949 to 1951, may have been created as part of a campaign to promote peace conferences in Sweden and Poland. The TGP artists Pablo O'Higgins, Leopoldo Méndez, Marianna Yampolsky, Adolfo Mexiac, and Francisco Mora composed large portfolios to decry the nuclear arma-

ment of world nations. In *Resistencia*, Méndez brings together images of the working class from many countries, united against fascism as symbolized by the soldier in the foreground. The figure on the ground may be a metaphor for the innocent victims of political aggression.

The main figure in *No Queremos la Guerra* symbolizes all the working people of the world who protest the threat of atomic war. This individual presents petitions reading "All the people of the world sign against the atomic war" to the world leaders planning nuclear warfare, who are reduced in size at the left of the composition.

PLATE 27
Unidad de Trabajo del Programa de Ruiz Cortines
Working Unit around the Program of Ruiz Cortines
1953
Adolfo Mexiac, Mexican, 1927–
Linocut, 29.5 x 22 inches (74.93 x 55.9 cm)
Gift of Charles S. Hayes '65
2009.012.032

This print epitomizes Mexiac's well-known imagery of friendship and solidarity. Here, members of the Federación de los Trabajadores del Distrito Federal march together in support of Ruiz Cortines, who was president of Mexico from 1952 to 1958. A banner in the background reads, "for the increase of wages" —referring to just one of Cortines's many initiatives to help the working class. As he took the presidential oath on December 1, 1952, Cortines swore, "I will not permit the principles of the Revolution or the laws that guide us to be broken."[58] One of the president's major achievements was in the area of women's rights: he gave women the right to vote in all Mexican elections.[59] Thus, although he ruled years after the Mexican Revolution, Cortines continued to implement its ideals while looking toward the future.

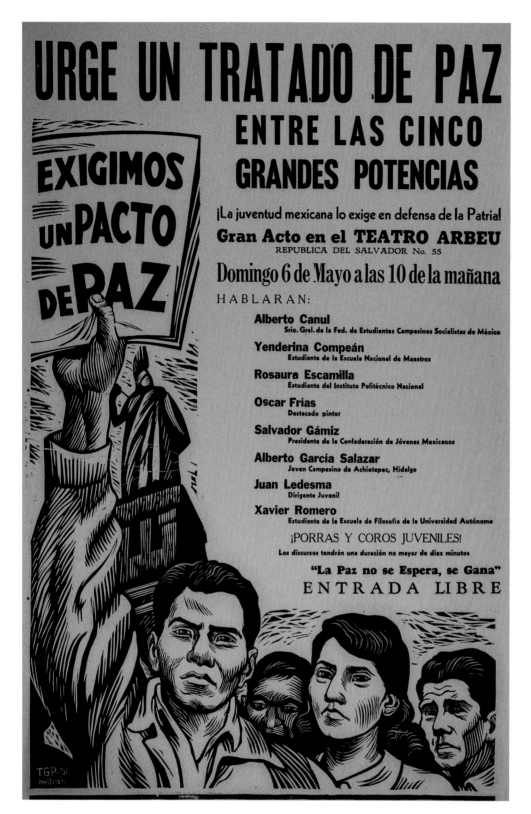

PLATE 28

Un Tratado Urgente de Paz Entre los Cinco Grandes
An Urgent Treaty of Peace between the Big Five
1951
Alberto Beltrán, Mexican, 1923–2002
Linocut, 31.75 x 20.5 (80.65 x 52.07 cm)
Gift of Charles S. Hayes '65
2009.008.002

In this poster advocating a peace treaty among the Big Five, the influence of Beltrán's former employment as a comic strip illustrator is clearly evident in his skillful blending of text and image. The Big Five countries—the United States, the United Kingdom, the USSR, China, and France—formed a council after World War II in the hope of drawing up peace treaties with former Axis countries. Although they held more than thirty meetings to achieve this, they only reached a stalemate.[60] Beltrán's poster advertises a meeting of Mexico City's youth, listing the names of various students scheduled to speak in demand of peace. The exigency of their request, visualized in the artist's broad, forceful cuts into the printing plate, is further amplified by the fact that this poster was produced six years after the meetings of the Big Five began.

PLATE 29
Ladrillero
Brick-Maker
1946
Pablo O'Higgins, American, 1904–1983
Lithograph, 14 x 11.25 inches (35.6 x 28.6 cm)
Gift of Charles S. Hayes '65
2009.007.116.E

Ladrillero exemplifies the style and subject matter typical of O'Higgins's work. Reminiscent of Honoré Daumier's scenes of peasants, the print demonstrates the loose, rhythmic line that activates O'Higgins's surfaces and brings movement to his figures. A man and a young boy each take on an equal share of work stacking bricks. O'Higgins monumentalizes the figures, instilling their otherwise humble task with noble dignity.

BUENOS VECINOS, BUENOS AMIGOS

TALLER DE GRAFICA POPULAR 1944

PLATE 30
Buenos Vecinos, Buenos Amigos
Good Neighbors, Good Friends
1944
Pablo O'Higgins, American 1904–1983
Linoleum cut, 18.13 x 25.25 inches (46.04 x 64.14 cm)
Gift of Charles S. Hayes '65
2009.008.013

The state of international relations between Mexico and the United States in the early 1940s is reflected in this print, which depicts Benito Juárez (Mexican president, 1861–63 and 1867–72) and Abraham Lincoln (United States president, 1861–65) in front of their respective national flags. Although no historical evidence suggests a political friendship between Juárez and Lincoln, their kinship as liberators of the common man had become symbolic of accord between the neighboring countries.[61] Between the depictions of the presidents in O'Higgins's print, two figures representing the working classes of Mexico and the United States shake hands in a gesture of goodwill.

O'Higgins uses this "historic" unifying iconography to express the current attitude of the Mexican Communist movement, which corresponded with that of the TGP, toward the United States. Since the end of the Stalin-Hitler pact and the establishment of the Sixth Period of the Communist International in 1941, the Taller had begun to engage more with the capitalist United States. Members of the workshop actively participated in Franklin D. Roosevelt's Good Neighbor Policy during the years of World War II.[62] Designed to create an open, positive exchange between the United States and Latin America, the cultural programs of the Good Neighbor program allowed the TGP artists to make connections with American artists, particularly in New York and Chicago. O'Higgins's print symbolizes the Taller's interest in establishing a dialogue with like-minded artists across the border.

La USRS Defiende las Libertades del Mundo. ¡AYUDEMOSLA!

PLATE 31

La USSR está Defendiendo la Libertad del Mundo. ¡Ayudémosla!
The USSR is Defending the Freedom of the World. Let's Help!
1941
Alfredo Zalce, Mexican, 1908–2003
Lithograph, 17.5 x 23 inches (44.45 x 58.42 cm)
Gift of Charles S. Hayes '65
2009.012.012

In this large poster from 1941 exhorting the Mexican public to help the USSR "defend the freedom of the world," Zalce's chaotic, caricatured style gives way to a bold, clear approach. Unlike his smaller, more complex posters such as the *Risa del Pueblo* (plate 12), this print was meant to be read in an instant by working-class Mexicans. There is no sarcasm or dark comedy to convey an unjust situation, simply a call to action.

Zalce's lithograph reflects the international, rather than domestic, concerns of the TGP. Indeed, the function of this poster is to promote an international proletariat against the common enemy of fascism—in this case, creating a particular bond with the USSR. Explaining this bond in an interview commenting on Leopoldo Méndez's visit to Moscow, TGP member Marianna Yampolsky stated, "The references in all of the talks were about the twin or sisterly feeling between the two groups—the one in the Soviet Union and the one in Mexico."[63] The emphatic ¡*Ayudémosla*!, or "Let's Help," also connotes a sense of unity within Mexican society. The Soviet *agitprop* poster movement of the 1920s was a particularly apparent source of influence for this lithograph, as for all of the TGP's propagandistic posters. Zalce would most certainly have looked to examples of these Soviet posters in creating his own iconography of the soldier heroically poised to defend against the implied threat of fascism.

PLATE 32
Matarlos en el Calor
To Kill Them in the Heat
1947
Alfredo Zalce, Mexican, 1908–2003
Linoleum cut, 12.19 x 8.13 inches (30.95 x 20.64 cm)
Gift of Charles S. Hayes '65
2009.007.075

Matarlos en el Calor (plate 32) and *El Criminal, Victoriano Huerta, Se Aduena del Poder* (plate 33) are two of the images that Alfredo Zalce contributed to the folio *Estampas de la Revolución Mexicana*. The two prints in the Charles S. Hayes collection, however, were not produced for the published book. They are printed on thicker white paper, whereas the published series was printed on rather thin multicolored paper. These two editions were most likely made before the establishment of the TGP publishing company and the publication of the *Estampas*.

The *Estampas's* historical outline tracing the revolution and its aftermath was intended to strengthen the legacy of President Lázaro Cárdenas and his successors in the Partido Revolucionario Institucional, the current ruling party. In its iconography, this collection of prints champions the politics of the Frente Popular de Cardenismo, around which the members of the TGP had rallied during the presidential campaign of Miguel Alemán Valdés.[64] Indeed, the government endorsed this project, printing the *Estampas* in the official party newspaper, *El Nacional*, in a three-month serial and thereby affording the TGP its largest audience to date.[65]

In *Matarlos en el Calor*, (plate 32) Zalce recounts the events surrounding the Veracruz Massacre of 1879, condemning Porfirio Díaz for his tyranny and betrayal.[66] In order to ameliorate the Mexican economy, President Díaz had made a law that redefined smuggling as a penal offense. This law caused unrest in Veracruz, and an unsigned telegram written in cipher was sent to the state's military governor, General Mier y Terán, instructing him to "Kill them in the heat." The general obeyed the order (thought to have been sent by Díaz), executing an estimated nine to fifteen people.[67]

Zalce presents the episode in two registers. In the top level, he has created a stoic portrait of the instigators of the massacre. Porfirio Díaz, recognizable from his distinctive moustache, is dressed in full regalia, gripping his sword and donning a plumed hat and medals. The expressions of the figures are indifferent; indeed, the only hints of the events shown below are the telegram reading *"Matalos en caliente"* in Díaz's hand and the sinister figure, presumably of Mier y Terán, who glares out from under the dark shadow of his hood. Below, a predella-like register vividly depicts the gruesome consequences of Díaz's order. By contrasting the horrific actions of shooting, whipping, hanging, and stabbing with the detached portrait above, Zalce effectively places condemnatory blame on Díaz and his conspirators.

El Criminal, Victoriano Huerta, Se Aduena del Poder (plate 33) exemplifies the morbid cynicism typical of Zalce's work. This print portrays the dictator Victoriano Huerta sitting in an imposing chair, with a menacing army of men bearing knives, guns, and rifles behind him and two men lying slain at his feet.[68] Zalce creates an effectively pernicious and malevolent characterization of Huerta by surrounding him with shadowy figures that look out at the viewer. Huerta had usurped the Mexican government from President Francisco Madero, who was subsequently murdered—a fate that many rivals of Huerta shared.[69] Zalce depicts the dictator as a drunkard, with legs crossed and eyelids drooping. Already inebriated, he grips his throne with his right hand and holds a bottle in his left —a visual expression of his immorality and unjust usurpation of power.

PLATE 33
El Criminal, Victoriano Huerta, Se Aduena del Poder
The Criminal, Victoriano Huerta, Takes Possession of Power
1941
Alfredo Zalce, Mexican, 1908–2003
Linoleum cut, 11.5 x 8.19 inches (29.2 x 20.79 cm)
Gift of Charles S. Hayes '65
2009.007.077

Para la Gente

PLATE 34
La Prensa al Servicio del Imperialismo
The Press Serving Imperialism
1946
Alfredo Zalce, Mexican, 1908–2003
Lithograph, 13.5 x 12 inches (34.29 x 30.5 cm)
Gift of Charles S. Hayes '65
2009.010.007

Following the decrease in political engagement that marked the TGP's activities after the end of President Cárdenas's administration, the 1946 elections gave the group an opportunity to support a political candidate and reassert their interest in social concerns. With no other likely leftist candidate, the TGP threw their support to Miguel Alemán, who would serve as president from 1946 to 1952. Alemán's presidency allowed the workshop to restore its relationship with the ruling party of the Mexican government and once again legitimized them to create politically critical prints.[70]

Alfredo Zalce created *La Prensa al Servicio del Imperialismo* at the dawn of this new political atmosphere. The print condemns the press's support of imperialist and fascist governments. Imperialism is represented as a monstrous, anthropomorphic balloon plastered with newspapers—the *Universal, El hombre libre, La prensa, Excelsior*, and *Omega*. By identifying specific, well-known papers, Zalce derogates the authority of the press in the mind of the viewer. As Imperialism rises over the figures below who inflate him with multiple pumps, he waves a menacing fascist salute. Zalce enhances the threat imposed by this monster by girding him with a bandolier and setting him against a dense, vertiginous sky. Typical of Zalce's work, the other figures also have grotesquely exaggerated physiognomies. Their bulging eyes and gaping mouths embody the artist's vilification of the press and the supporters of imperialism. Through *La prensa*, not only does Zalce support the ideals of the new presidency but he also reestablishes the TGP as the true "press" of the Mexican people.

PLATE 36
Lo Que No Puedo Venir
That Which Must Not Come
1945
Leopoldo Méndez, Mexican, 1902–1969
Woodcut, 11.88 x 6.88 inches (30.2 x 17.5 cm)
Gift of Charles S. Hayes '65
2009.007.022

Executed in 1945, toward the end of World War II, Méndez's *Lo Que No Puede Venir* (plate 36) is a complex self-portrait commissioned by Carl O. Schniewind for his 1945 exhibition at the AIC. Schniewind had previously gone to Mexico to visit the TGP, purchasing works by several artists with the intention of exhibiting them back in Chicago. Méndez created this piece for Schniewind while working in Chicago.

Méndez produced only three self-portraits during his lifetime, this being the first. The imagery in this woodcut uses one of the denser schemes he had employed to date. We see the artist in the lower portion of the print, lying on a sea of portfolios by Posada. Seemingly lost in a daydream, he writes his name and the year, 1945, on the top page. Deborah Caplow, in her study of Méndez's work, observes that "this is not only a portrait of Mendéz but also a portrayal of Mexico at a precise moment in history at the end of World War II... The artist lies in front of a wall of cactus, from which we see emerge a rattlesnake and cross with an eagle crucified hanging from it, its wings pinned by crossed daggers. Blades in the shape of a swastika extend from the four directions of the cross."[71] The variety of images and symbols that Méndez includes are drawn from pre-Columbian iconography and nineteenth-century cultural history. By using them here within the context of a self-portrait, he situates himself and his fellow artists within the heady political climate of Mexico City at the end of World War II.[72]

PLATE 37
Mujer y Niño
Woman and Boy
1942
Eleanor Coen, American, 1916–
Color lithograph, 13.25 x 7.5 inches (33.7 x 19.1 cm)
Gift of Charles S. Hayes '65
2009.020.002

Para la Gente

CONGRESO CONTINENTAL AMERICANO POR LA PAZ
MEXICO, 5-10 DE SEPTIEMBRE, 1949

Colaboración del TALLER DE GRAFICA POPULAR, México, D. F.

GANAREMOS LA PAZ
SI LUCHAMOS POR ELLA

PLATE 38
Cartel para el Congreso Continental Americano para la
Paz (Ganaremos la Paz si Luchamos por Ella)
Poster for the American Continental Congress for Peace
(We Will Win the Peace if We Fight for It)
1949
Arturo Garcia Bustos and Mariana Yampolsky
Mexican, 1926–; American, 1925–2002
Linocut, 29.13 x 22.63 inches (74 x 57.5 cm)
Gift of Charles S. Hayes '65
2009.012.025

Along with fellow TGP artists Alberto Beltrán and Arturo
Garcia Bustos, Mariana Yampolsky worked for one
year as an apprentice to Pablo O'Higgins and Alfredo
Zalce. This poster is an example of her early work with
Bustos. It was created for the Continental American
Congress for Peace in Mexico City in September 1949.
The work is typical of the posters the Taller created for
rallies, conferences, organized demonstrations, and
other gatherings for social or political causes. Here, a
Mexican peasant family is set in the foreground of the
image. The mother holds an infant child as the father
confronts the swords of the militia, his sledgeham-
mer raised to defend his family. This type of subject
matter became emblematic of the TGP and their work.

PLATE 39
Campesinos
Peasants
Date unknown
Elizabeth Catlett, African American, 1919–
Linocut, 7.13 x 5.13 inches (18.1 x 13 cm)
Gift of Charles S. Hayes '65
2009.018.026

This linocut celebrates the noble dignity of the *campesinos* (peasants). Catlett elevates their mundane tasks and celebrates their importance to the social fabric of the culture. Many of her works with the Taller referenced popular photographic images of the Mexican people, images that would have been immediately recognizable to the primarily illiterate Mexican working class. Catlett's moving prints, commenting on the exigencies of the human condition, gained her the Art Institute of Chicago's first Legends and Legacy Award in 2005.[23]

ENDNOTES

01 Donald J. Mabry, "Cárdenas del Río, Lázaro (1895–1970)," *Historical Text Archive*, http://historicaltextarchive.com/sections.php?op=viewarticle&artid=132"http://historicaltextarchive.com/sections.php?op=viewarticle&artid=132.

02 I am indebted to Joe Segura, master printmaker and head of Segura Publishing Company, in Tempe, Arizona, and Nancy Heller, daughter of Jules and Gloria Heller, for their permission to print a transcript of interviews Segura conducted with the Hellers several years ago.

03 James M. Wechsler, "Propaganda Grafica," in John Ittmann, ed., *Mexico and Modern Printmaking: A Revolution in the Graphic Arts, 1920 to 1950*, with contributions by Shoemaker, Innis H., James Wechsler, and Lyle W. Williams. Exhibition catalog, Philadelphia Museum of Art and McNay Art Museum (New Haven: Yale University Press, 2006), 68.

04 Hannes Meyer, *TGP México: El Taller de Gráfica Popular; Doce años de obra artística colectiva* (Mexico City: La Estampa Mexicana, 1949): 18.

05 Alison McClean-Cameron, "El Taller de Gráfica Popular: Printmaking and Politics in Mexico and Beyond, from the Popular Front to the Cuban Revolution" (PhD diss., University of Essex, 2000), 236–38.

06 Laura Caldwell, *The Handbook of Texas Online*, s.v. "Madero, Francisco Indalecio," http://www.tshaonline.org/handbook/online/articles/MM/fmaad_print.html" http://www.tshaonline.org/handbook/online/articles/MM/fmaad_print.html.

07 *Encyclopaedia Britannica*, 2009 edition, s.v. "Obregón, Álvaro."

08 Diana Miliotes, *José Guadalupe Posada and the Mexican Broadside* (Chicago: Art Institute of Chicago, 2006), 9.

09 The Chicano art movement grew out of the Civil Rights Movement of the 1970s in Los Angeles. It sought to gain social equality for Mexican Americans and to reclaim and educate them of their rich heritage. This political activism and renewed cultural pride were expressed in Chicano visual art, music, literature, dance, theater, and other forms of expression. The movement developed within of the same kind of political and social climate that brought the TGP artists together.

10 In this, I am enormously grateful to Gerta Katz for the hours of phone interviews I conducted with her. Gerta and her husband, Samuel, were close friends with many TGP artists, working and traveling with them in Mexico. The core of the Charles S. Hayes Collection is from the Samuel and Gerta Katz TGP Collection. I am also grateful to Noah and Katie Kahn for their recollections of their parents, Max Kahn and Eleanor Coen, and the time they spent in both Chicago and Mexico, working with the Taller. TGP artists Arturo Garciá Bustos and Jesús Álvarez Amaya generously provided video interviews, which were a rich resource. Colleagues in Mexico and the United States also kindly provided me with information and recollections of their time working with artists Jules Heller, Milton Rogovin, Alfredo Zalce, Marianna Yampolsky, and others.

11 For a fuller discussion of the Weyhe Gallery and its relationship with Mexican artists during the 1920s and onward, consult Innes Howe Shoemaker, "Crossing Borders: The Weyhe Gallery and the Vogue for Mexican Art in the United States, 1926–40," in Ittmann, Mexico and Modern Printmaking, 27–29.

12 Cheryl Ganz and Margaret Strobel, eds., *Pots of Promise: Mexicans and Pottery at Hull-House, 1920–40* (Urbana, IL: University of Illinois Press with the Jane Addams Hull-House Museum, 2004), 94.

13 These details were shared with me by Coen and Kahn's children, Noah and Katie Kahn.

14 McClean-Cameron, "El Taller de Gráfica Popular," 169.

15 Rene Arco shared this information with me in a May 28, 2008, e-mail recounting his recollections of working with Zalce as a print student.

16 Meyer, *TGP México*, 50.

17 Meyer, *TGP México*, 72.

18 Jules Heller, *Codex Méndez: Prints by Leopoldo Méndez (1902–1969)*, ed. Jean Makin (Tempe, AZ: Arizona State University Art Museum, 1999).

19 McClean-Cameron, "El Taller de Gráfica Popular," 189.

20 Graphic Witness Visual Arts and Social Commentary, "Francisco Mora (1922–2002)," *Graphicwitness.org*, http://www.graphicwitness.org/group/tgpmora2.htm"

21 Meyer, *TGP México*, 102.

22 Carlos Merida and Frances Toor, *Modern Mexican Artists: Critical Notes* (Mexico City: Frances Toor Studios: 1937), 121.

23 Deborah Caplow, *Leopoldo Méndez: Revolutionary Art and the Mexican Print* (Austin: University of Texas Press, 2007), 81.

24 Virginia Stewart, *45 Contemporary Mexican Artists: A Twentieth-Century Renaissance* (Stanford, CA: Stanford University Press, 1951), 87–88.

25 Bertha Taracena and Alfredo Zalce, *Alfredo Zalce: Un arte proprio* (Mexico City: Universidad Nacional Autonoma de Mexico, Dirección General de Difusión Cultural, 1984), 82.

26 Merida and Toor, *Modern Mexican Artists*, 201.

27 Taracena and Zalce, *Alfredo Zalce*, 83.

28 McClean-Cameron, "El Taller de Gráfica Popular," 215. McClean-Cameron discusses the proletarian identity and the influence of German and Soviet poster workshops on the TGP.

29 Ittmann, *Mexico and Modern Printmaking*, 222–23.

30 David Craven, Art and Revolution in Latin America, 1910–1990 (New Haven: Yale University Press, 2006), 67.

31 Ittmann, Mexico and Modern Printmaking, 200.

32 New Jersey Hong Kong Network, "Basic Facts on the Nanjinh Massacre and the Tokyo War Crimes Trial," *My China News Digest*, http://www.cnd.org/njmassacre/nj.html.

33 NationMaster, "Encyclopedia: Stalin Peace Prize," *NationMaster.com*, http://www.nationmaster.com/encyclopedia/Stalin-Peace-Prize.

34 Caplow, *Leopoldo Méndez*, 216.

35 McClean-Cameron, "El Taller de Gráfica Popular," 103.

36 Franklin Rosemont, "Spanish Revolution of 1936," The Center for Programs in Creative Writing, University of Pennsylvania, http://www.writing.upenn.edu/ffafilreis/88/spain-overview.html.

37 Antonio Turok, master photographer, personal communication, November 21, 2008.

[38] Ittmann, *Mexico and Modern Printmaking*, 217.

[39] Ricardo Donato Salvatore, Carlos Aguirre, and G. M. Joseph, *Crime and Punishment in Latin America: Law and Society since Late Colonial Times* (Durham, NC: Duke University Press: 2001), 256.

[40] Raquel Sosa Elìzaga, *Los còdigos ocultos del Cardenismo: Un estudio de la violencia politica, el cambio social y la continuidad institucional* (Mexico City: Universidad Nacional Autónoma de México, 1996).

[41] For article 123, see Cámara de Diputados, Legislatura XXXVII—Año II—Período Ordinario—Fecha 19381108—Número de Diario 12: "Acta de la sesión celebrada por la Cámara de Diputados del XXXVII Congreso de la Unión, el día ocho de noviembre de mil novecientos treinta y ocho," 8 Noviembre 1938, http://cronica.diputados.gob.mx/DDebates/37/2do/Ord/19381108.html". For Article 127, see Marc Becker, "Mexico: 1917 Constitution (Becker version)," *Historical Text Archive*, "http://historicaltextarchive.com/sections.php?op=viewarticle&artid=123".

[42] The *Indice* reads, "Francisco I Madero recorre el pais para hacer del conocimiento popular su programa de Gobierno. Como candidato a la Presidencia de la Republica capta todas los problemas de Mexico. A fines de 1911, como resultado de una votacion libre y espontanea, assume la Primera Magistratura del pais. El licenciado Jose Maria Pino Suarez es electo Vicepresidente de la Republica. Bajo el Gobierno maderista, las libertades son una grandiosa realidad."

[43] Martin Donell Kohout, *The Handbook of Texas Online*, s.v. "Huerta, Victoriano," http://www.tshaonline.org/handbook/online/articles/HH/fhu81.html.

[44] Michael S. Werner, ed., *The Concise Encyclopedia of Mexico* (Chicago: Fitzroy Dearborn, 2001), 70.

[45] Antonio Turok, personal communication, November 21, 2008.

[46] Caplow, *Leopoldo Méndez*, 147.

[47] Turok, personal communication, November 21, 2008.

[48] Jaymie Heilman, "The Demon Inside: Madre Conchita, Gender, and the Assassination of Obregón," *Mexican Studies* 18, no. 1 (2002): 23–60.

[49] Bamber Gascoigne, "History of Mexico. Revolution: AD 1910–1920," *HistoryWorld*, www.historyworld.net/wrldhis/PlainTextHistories.asp?ParagraphID=nxp.

[50] Susan Valerie Richards, "Imaging the Political: El Taller de Gráfica Popular in Mexico, 1937–1949" (PhD diss., The University of New Mexico, 2001), 162–64.

[51] Alfredo Zalce, interview by Sam Allred, 2002, "http://www.zalce.com/zalce/gran_ciudad.html" http://www.zalce.com/zalce/gran_ciudad.html.

[52] This print came into the Hayes Collection directly from the children of Chicago artists Eleanor Coen and Max Kahn. Coen and Kahn were close friends of Zalce and acquired this print, as well as several others by the artist, while working with the Taller in Mexico City.

[53] McClean-Cameron, "El Taller de Gráfica Popular," 63.

[54] Alicia Azuela, "*El Machete and Frente a Frente: Art Committed to Social Justice in Mexico*," Art Journal 52, no. 1 (Spring 1993): 82–87.

[55] Caplow, *Leopoldo Méndez*, 177–81.

[56] Ibid. Caplow notes that El Zopilote's attributes of a top hat and coat suggest that he represents capitalism and imperialism.

[57] Ibid., 174–76.

[58] Enrique Krauze, *Mexico: Biography of Power; A History of Modern Mexico*, 1810–1996 (New York: Harper Collins, 1997), 601.

[59] Ibid., 613.

[60] George Novack, "The Big Five at London," *Fourth International* 6, no. 11 (November 1945): 333–36.

[61] Leonard Gordon, "Lincoln and Juarez—A Brief Reassessment of Their Relationship," *The Hispanic American Historical Review* (Duke University Press) 48, no. 1 (February 1968): 75–80.

[62] McClean-Cameron, "El Taller de Gráfica Popular," 265.

[63] Ibid., 215.

[64] Ibid., 132–34.

[65] Ibid., 142.

[66] Alberto Morales Jiménez provides this description of the massacre in the *Indice de los Grabados con Notas Historicas* in the *Estampas de la Revolución Mexicana*: " '¡MATALOS EN CALIENTE! VERACRUZ, 25 DE JUNIO DE 1879.' Grabado de Alfredo Zalce. 'Aprehendidos infraganti, mátalos en caliente,' decia el telegrama que Porfirio Díaz envoi al general Luis Mier y Terán, Comandante Militar de Veracruz, para indicarle que, sin juicio, fusilara a varias persona cuyo único delito consista en anhelar un regimen democrático. El 25 de junio de 1879 fueron llevados al paredón los jefes de este frustrado movimiento revolucionario, precursor de los acontecimentos de 1910."

[67] John H. Seward, "The Veracruz Massacre of 1879," *The Americas* (Academy of American Franciscan History) 32, no. 4 (April 1976): 585–96.

[68] Alberto Morales Jiménez provides this description of Huerta in the *Indice de los Grabados con Notas Historicas*: " 'EL CRIMINAL VICTORIANO HUERTA DE ADUEÑA DEL PODER. 19 DE FEBRERO DE 1913.' Grabado de Alfredo Zalce. El dipsómano Victoriano Huerta llega al Palacio Nacional y se hace nombrar Presidente de la Republica. Colaboran con él José Maria Rozano, Querido Moheno, Nemesio Garcia Naranjo, Olaguíbel y otros intelectuales reaccionarios. Por fortuna, la usurpació se levanta en armas para encarrilar nuevamente al país por senderos constitucionales."

[69] George J. Rausch, Jr., "The Exile and Death of Victoriano Huerta," *The Hispanic American Historical Review* (Duke University Press) 42, no. 2 (May 1962): 133.

[70] McClean-Cameron, "El Taller de Gráfica Popular," 118–127.

[71] Caplow, *Leopoldo Méndez*, 185.

[72] Ibid.

[73] Melanie Anne Herzog, *Elizabeth Catlett: In the Image of the People*, exhibition catalog, Art Institute of Chicago (Chicago: Art Institute of Chicago; New Haven: distributed by Yale University Press, 2005), 7.

Becker, Heather. *Art for the People: The Rediscovery and Preservation of Progressive and WPA-Era Murals in the Chicago Public Schools, 1904–1943*. San Francisco: Chronicle Books, 2002.

Caplow, Deborah. Leopoldo Méndez: *Revolutionary Art and the Mexican Print*. Austin: University of Texas Press, 2007.

Craven, David. *Art and Revolution in Latin America, 1910–1990*. New Haven: Yale University Press, 2006.

Delpar, Helen. *The Enormous Vogue of Things Mexican: Cultural Relations between the United States and Mexico, 1920–1935*. Tuscaloosa, AL: The University of Alabama Press, 1992.

Freeman, Rachel, and Diane Miliotes. *José Guadalupe Posada and the Mexican Broadside. Exhibition catalog, Art Institute of Chicago*. Chicago: Art Institute of Chicago: 2006.

Ganz, Cheryl, and Margaret Strobel, eds. *Pots of Promise: Mexicans and Pottery at Hull House, 1920–40*. Urbana, IL: University of Illinois Press with the Jane Addams Hull-House Museum, 2004.

García de Germenos, Pilar, and James Oles, eds. *Gritos desde el archivo: Grabado político del taller de gráfica popular, Colección Academia de Artes (Shouts from the Archive: Political Prints from the Taller de Gráfica Popular, Accademy of Arts Collection)*. Mexico City: Colección Blaisten / Centro Cultural Universitario Tlatelolco, 2008.

Goldman, Shifra M. *Contemporary Mexican Painting in a Time of Change*. Austin: University of Texas Press, 1981.

———. *Dimensions of the Americas: Art and Social Change in Latin America and the United States*. Chicago: The University of Chicago Press, 1994.

Haab, Armin, and C. C. Palmer. *Mexican Graphic Art*. New York: G. Wittenborn, 1957.

Heilman, Jaymie. "The Demon Inside: Madre Conchita, Gender, and the Assassination of Obregón." *Mexican Studies* 18, no. 1 (2002): 23–60.

Heller, Jules. *Codex Méndez: Prints by Leopoldo Méndez (1902–1969)*, edited by Jean Makin. Tempe, AZ: Arizona State University Art Museum, 1999.

———. *Printmaking Today: An Introduction to the Graphic Arts*. New York: Holt, 1958.

Hemingway, Andrew. *Artists on the Left: American Artists and the Communist Movement, 1926–1956*. New Haven: Yale University Press, 2002.

Herzog, Melanie Anne. *Elizabeth Catlett: An American Artist in Mexico*. Seattle: University of Washington Press, 2005.

———. Elizabeth Catlett: *In the Image of the People. Exhibition catalog, Art Institute of Chicago. Chicago: Art Institute of Chicago*; New Haven: distributed by Yale University Press, 2005.

Ittmann, John W., ed. *Mexico and Modern Printmaking: A Revolution in the Graphic Arts, 1920 to 1950*. With contributions by Innis H. Shoemaker, James Wechsler, and Lyle W. Williams. Exhibition catalog, Philadelphia Museum of Art and McNay Art Museum. New Haven: Yale University Press, 2006.

Kennedy, Elizabeth, Wendy Greenhouse, Daniel Schulman, and Susan Weininger. *Chicago Modern, 1893–1945: Pursuit of the New*. Exhibition catalog, Terra Museum of American Art. Chicago: University of Chicago Press, 2004.

Koch, Peter Rutledge, Richard Seibert, Max Koch, Adán Griego, and D. Vanessa Kam. *José Guadalupe Posada and the Taller De Gráfica Popular: Mexican Popular Prints; Published on the Occasion of the Exhibition at the Stanford University Libraries*, November 1, 2002–March 15, 2003. Stanford, CA: The Stanford University Libraries, 2002.

Krauze, Enrique. *Mexico: Biography of Power; A History of Modern Mexico, 1810–1996*. New York: Harper Collins, 1997.

LeFalle-Collins, Lizzetta, and Shifra M. Goldman. *In the Spirit of Resistance: African-American Modernists and the Mexican Muralist School (En el espíritu de la resistencia: Modernistas Africanoamericanos y la escuela muralista)*. New York: American Federation of Arts, 1996.

MacGregor, Josefina. *Revolución y diplomacia: México y España, 1913–1917*. Colección Premio Salvador Azuela. Mexico City: Instituto Nacional de Estudios Históricos de la Revolución Mexicana, 2002.

McClean-Cameron, Alison. "El Taller de Gráfica Popular: Printmaking and Politics in Mexico and Beyond, from the Popular Front to the Cuban Revolution." PhD diss., University of Essex, 2000.

Méndez, Leopoldo, and Carlos Monsiváis. *Leopoldo Méndez y su tiempo: Colección Carlos Monsiváis; El privilegio del dibujo*. Mexico City: Instituto Nacional de Bellas Artes, 2002.

Para la Gente

Mercado, Dolores, Marilyn Lara Corral, Samantha Castro, and Angelina Villanueva. *Women Artists of Modern Mexico: Frida's Contemporaries (Mujeres artistas en el México de la modernidad: Las contemporáneas de Frida)*. Chicago: National Museum of Mexican Art, 2008.

Mérida, Carlos, and Frances Toor. *Modern Mexican Artists: Critical Notes*. Mexico City: Frances Toor Studios, 1937.

Mexican Fine Arts Center. *Prints of the Mexican Masters (Grabados de los maestros Mexicanos)*. Chicago: Mexican Fine Arts Center, 1987.

Meyer, Hannes. *TGP México: El Taller de Gráfica Popular; Doce años de obra artistica colectiva*. Mexico City: La Estampa Mexicana, 1949.

Meyer, Michael C. *Huerta: A Political Portrait*. Lincoln, NE: University of Nebraska Press, 1972.

Michael Rosenfeld Gallery. *Charles White: Let the Light Enter; Major Drawings, 1942–1969*. New York: Michael Rosenfeld Gallery, 2009.

Musacchio, Humberto. *El taller de gráfica popular*. Mexico City: Fondo de Cultura Económica, 2007.

Novack, George. "The Big Five at London," *Fourth International* 6, no. 11 (November 1945): 333–36.

O'Shaughnessy, Edith. *Intimate Pages of Mexican History*. New York: George H. Doran, 1920.

Phagan, Patricia. *For the People: American Mural Drawings of the 1930s and 1940s*. Exhibition catalog, Frances Lehman Loeb Art Center, Vassar College. Poughkeepsie, NY: Frances Lehman Loeb Art Center, 2007.

Prignitz-Poda, Helga, and the Taller de Gráfica Popular. *El Taller de Gráfica Popular en México, 1937–1977*. Mexico City: Instituto Nacional de Bellas Artes, 1992.

Rausch, George J., Jr. "The Early Career of Victoriano Huerta." *The Hispanic American Historical Review* (Duke University Press) 42, no. 2 (October 1964): 136–45.

———. "The Exile and Death of Victoriano Huerta." *The Hispanic American Historical Review* (Duke University Press) 42, no. 2 (May 1962): 133–51.

Richards, Susan Valerie. "Imaging the Political: El Taller de Gráfica Popular in Mexico, 1937–1949." PhD diss., The University of New Mexico, 2001.

Ross, John, and Clare Romano. *The Complete Printmaker: The Art and Technique of the Relief Print, the Intaglio Print, the Collagraph, the Lithograph, the Screen Print, the Dimensional Print, Photographic Prints, Children's Prints, Collecting Prints, Print Workshop*. New York: Free Press, 1972.

Salvatore, Ricardo Donato, Carlos Aguirre, and G. M. Joseph. *Crime and Punishment in Latin America: Law and Society since Late Colonial Times*. Durham, NC: Duke University Press, 2001.

Sherman, William L., and Richard E. Greenleaf. *Victoriano Huerta: A Reappraisal*. Mexico City: Centro de Estudios Mexicanos, distributed by Mexico City College Press, 1960.

Sosa Elízaga, Raquel. *Los códigos ocultos del cardenismo: Un estudio de la violencia política, el cambio social y la continuidad institucional*. Mexico City: Universidad Nacional Autónoma de México, 1996.

Stewart, Virginia. *45 Contemporary Mexican Artists: A Twentieth-Century Renaissance*. Stanford, CA: Stanford University Press, 1951.

Sullivan, Edward J. *The Language of Objects in the Art of the Americas*. New Haven: Yale University Press, 2007.

Taller de Gráfica Popular. *Estampas de la Revolucion Mexicana: 85 grabados de los artistas del Taller de Gráfica Popular*. Mexico City: Editado por "La Estampa Mexicana," 1947.

Taracena, Berta, and Alfredo Zalce. *Alfredo Zalce: Un arte propio*. Mexico City: Universidad Nacional Autonoma de Mexico, Dirección General de Difusión Cultural, 1984.

Tuñón Pablos, Esperanza. *Huerta y el movimiento obrero*. Mexico City: Ediciones el Caballito, 1982.

Vaca, Alfonso, and Alfredo Zalce. *Alfredo Zalce*. Michoacán, Mexico: Gobierno del Estado de Michoacán, Secretaría de Cultura, 2005.

Werner, Michael S. *The Concise Encyclopedia of Mexico*. Chicago: Fitzroy Dearborn, 2001.

Yampolsky, Mariana, Mónica Lavín, and Elena Alvarez Buylla Roces. *Formas de vida: Plantas Mexicanas vistas por Mariana Yampolsky (Life forms: Mexican Plants as Seen by Mariana Yampolsky)*. Mexico City: Instituto Nacional de Ecología, 2003.

Zalce, Alfredo. *Alfredo Zalce: Artista Michoacano*. Morelia, Mexico: Gobierno del Estado de Michoacán, 1997.

COLOPHON

This catalog was printed by Evangel Press in Nappanee, Indiana
and The Papers Inc. Press in Milford, Indiana in June of 2009

Cover: Utopia Premium, Ivory, Silk, 110 lb. Cover
Body: Utopia Two, Ivory, Matte, 100 lb. Text
Typeface: Conduit ITC

Bound at Dekker Bookbinding in Grand Rapids, Michigan

Design and Production by Michael Swoboda, MA '08

Published by the Snite Museum of Art at the University of Notre Dame

Copyright 2009